WHAT
Happens
IN
VEGAS

WHAT Happens IN VEGAS

Sabrina Wagner

Stay Connected!

**Want to be the first to learn book news, updates and more?
Sign up for my Newsletter.**

https://www.subscribepage.com/sabrinawagnernewsletter

**Want to know about my new releases and upcoming sales?
Stay connected on:**

Facebook~Instagram~Twitter~TikTok
Goodreads~BookBub~Amazon

**I'd love to hear from you.
Visit my website to connect with me.**

www.sabrinawagnerauthor.com

Books by Sabrina Wagner

Hearts Trilogy
Hearts on Fire
Shattered Hearts
Reviving my Heart

Wild Hearts Trilogy
Wild Hearts
Secrets of the Heart
Eternal Hearts

Forever Inked Novels
Tattooed Hearts: Tattooed Duet #1
Tattooed Souls: Tattooed Duet #2
Smoke and Mirrors
Regret and Redemption
Sin and Salvation

Vegas Love Series
What Happens in Vegas
Billionaire Bachelor in Vegas

Spotify Playlist

Take My Breath~ The Weeknd
Toxic~ Britney Spears
Strangelove~ Depeche Mode
You Can Leave Your Hat On~ Joe Cocker
Way Down We Go~ KALEO
Sail~ AWOLNATION
Unsteady~ X Ambassadors
Can't Live Without You~ Owl City
Power~ Isak Danielson
Legendary~ Welshly Arms

Listen and Enjoy!

Prologue

"Redhead at the bar."

My eyes swung in that direction. She was hard to miss. Fiery-red hair that clearly wasn't natural, but stunning just the same, hung down to the middle of her back in soft waves. Silky locks any man would die to run his hands through.

But her hair was only the tip of the iceberg. She wore a flirty black dress that draped off her shoulders, baring a tattoo on her creamy skin. My eyes wandered down her body to her legs and the black stilettos that adorned her feet. One leg bobbed nervously where it crossed over the other.

"She'll do," I said to my friend without taking my eyes off the beauty. Women like her were my weakness. She had me wanting more, when one night was all I had to give.

"I'll take lead," he said, tossing back his whiskey.

I was on my feet with my suit coat buttoned before he swallowed. "I got it."

We'd been playing this game since college when a feisty coed showed us pleasure came in threes. Before that, I'd fantasized about a ménage à trois, but it always involved another woman, not my roommate. She schooled us that semester on how to please a woman in ways we hadn't even

1

imagined. Since then, we'd entertained lots of ladies with the skills we mastered. Great sex was about bringing a woman to orgasm many times over and seeing the look of pure ecstasy on her face. It was about being in the moment and treating her like a queen. Nothing was sexier than a woman who truly enjoyed herself.

I slipped onto the ornate stool next to hers at the bar. The Weeknd's "Take My Breath" played softly overhead. Of all the bars in Vegas, this was one of my favorites, and since I grew up here, I'd been to them all. I'd outgrown the dance clubs with their pulsing techno music and flashing lights. Sports bars weren't my thing, and I was too young to patronize cigar bars. This classy vibe, with its R&B songs better fit my persona.

"What can I get you?" the bartender asked.

"Macallan. Neat."

From the corner of my eye, I saw her brow lift as she sipped her martini. She was even more beautiful up close. Silky smooth skin, cherry-red lips, and winged eyeliner right out of the sixties. Throw her in a red polka-dot dress and she'd be an iconic pinup girl.

The bartender placed my glass on the granite bar top.

"Thank you." I took a small sip and turned to the siren next to me. "What's a woman like you doing here all alone?"

She finished her martini and held her empty glass toward the bartender. "Does that line usually work? Kind of cliché, don't you think?"

I chuckled at the woman for calling me out. "Fair enough, but still a valid question."

"Escaping… just like everyone else in Vegas." Her voice was strawberries drizzled in dark chocolate. Sweet with a hint of forbidden.

I glanced at her naked hand. "Husband?"

"No." She lifted her replenished glass to her lips.

"Boyfriend?"

"Not for a while now." She was giving me the cold shoulder, but I was determined to break through her icy demeanor.

"Is there a crazy bachelorette party you're trying to avoid?"

Her cherry-red lips turned up at the corners. "That one would actually make sense, but sadly no. I came to Vegas alone."

I was intrigued. "Coming to Sin City alone is a risky move. A beautiful woman like yourself is a walking target for an unscrupulous man trying to get into your panties."

She let out a laugh that ended with a snort and quickly covered it with her hand. It was fucking adorable. "Oh, my god. That was so embarrassing." She turned and faced me completely. "You wouldn't happen to be one of those unscrupulous men, would you?"

I licked my lips and her eyes zoned in on them. "My scruples are fully intact. I'll tell you no lies. I definitely want into your panties. That is, if you're wearing any."

She sucked in her cheeks as they flushed crimson. "And why would I let you do that? I don't know you. What if you're a serial killer who'll leave me dead for the maid to find?"

Now, I laughed. "Do I look dangerous to you?"

She tapped a red fingernail against her lips. "You may not be a serial killer, but you're definitely dangerous."

I leaned forward into her space. "The only danger is having the best orgasms of your life. A souvenir you'll be thinking about for months. Don't you think you deserve that?"

A visible shiver shook her body. "I don't even know your name."

I had her on the hook, I just needed to reel her in. "Names are unnecessary. One night is all I'm offering. After that, we go our separate ways. What's the point in coming to Sin City if you aren't willing to gamble? Everyone knows what happens in Vegas stays in Vegas. No strings. No attachments. Just pleasure."

Brett slid onto the stool on the other side of her and ran his fingers down her spine. "Double the pleasure."

Her head snapped his way. "Excuse me?"

"I was getting to that."

"Getting to what?" she asked, looking between us, and clearly confused at the situation.

Damn Brett for jumping the gun before I laid the necessary groundwork. I whispered in her ear, "Ever had a threesome before?"

Her breath hitched. "No."

3

I swept a lock of her fiery hair behind her ear. "We can make your wildest fantasies come true. Pleasure you didn't know existed."

Brett closed in on the other side with a kiss to her neck. "Imagine four hands all over this gorgeous body."

"Two mouths," I said seductively.

Brett went in for the kill. "Two cocks deep inside you."

She shivered again. "I'm not sure I can handle that."

"You can," I said. "The question is, will you roll the dice and take a chance on having the most erotic experience of your life?"

"You have all the control, baby. Two men to do your bidding. If at any point you want to stop, all you have to do is say no, but I can guarantee that word won't cross your lips." Brett was a smooth talker. He closed deals all over the country, with both multibillion-dollar companies and lovely ladies. He had a charm about him women couldn't resist.

I could see the wheels spinning in her pretty little head. Weighing her options. Deciding if this was something she wanted to do. "You've got nothing to lose and everything to gain."

"What about my self-respect?"

"You're in Vegas. Everyone is involved in their own debauchery. No one needs to know. When you leave, we can be your dirty little secret," Brett said.

The column of her throat bobbed as she swallowed down her apprehension. "I can leave at any time?"

"You can, but you won't want to." I stood and took her hand, leading her across the marble tile and over to the elevators as Brett paid the tab. I stared at our reflection in the gold doors as we waited for them to open. We looked good together. If she wasn't a tourist breezing through the city, I might have been tempted to spend more than one night with her.

The doors opened and I led her inside. With her back to my chest, I wrapped my arms gently around her full hips and nuzzled into her neck. "Are you nervous?"

"Yes," she whispered.

"Don't be. We'll take very good care of you. Trust me."

4

Chapter 1
Gia

I looked in the mirror and straightened my green sheath dress. It was classy but understated and perfect for the first day of my new life. My red hair was pulled back into a French twist and my lips colored with a hint of gloss. Professional. That was the look I was going for.

Moving to Las Vegas was a risk, but one I needed to take. Escaping from Waukegan had to happen. The only thing that made living there bearable was my job in Chicago where I worked as an event coordinator for a prestigious hotel. Despite its impressive status, I still never earned enough money to move to the city, and the almost hour drive was killing me. And my family... I loved them, I really did... but moving home after a failed marriage just about did me in.

I needed a complete makeover and what better place to reinvent yourself than Vegas. When the internal memo came about this position, I didn't hesitate to apply. I quickly filled out the application, attached my résumé, and hit send before I could change my mind. The next day I had a video interview with Mr. Dorsey and the job was mine.

One of the best parts of moving to Vegas was the suite I'd be calling home for the next year in the very same hotel, Mystique, where I now worked. It was convenient and paid for.

I grabbed my knockoff Prada bag, made my way to the elevator, and pushed the button for the second floor where my new office was, putting aside any thoughts of my illicit affair from Friday. It was a one-time thing and I'd never see them again. *Thank goodness!* In the light of day my poor judgment glared like the neon lights of the Strip. It was stupid and reckless, yet I didn't regret it as much as I thought I would. Never in my life had I experienced such pure bliss.

The doors opened to an elaborate lobby. My heels clicked loudly as I crossed the shiny tile floor to the reception desk.

"May I help you?"

"I'm Gianna Romano. I'm…" I started.

She stood and reached her hand out. "Of course. You're our new event coordinator. I'm Teresa."

I shook her hand. "Nice to meet you." I took in the lavish lobby decorated in black and silver with a few pops of deep, bold color. "This place is spectacular."

"It's Mystique. Nothing but the best for our guests and employees." She motioned to the room around us. "We're very excited to have you join our team. Unfortunately, our last event coordinator left abruptly, and you couldn't have arrived at a better time." She reached behind the desk and pulled out a lanyard with a key card attached. "That will get you into the offices." She pointed at the frosted glass doors behind her. "Let me call Penny to show you around. She'll be your personal assistant."

"Thank you, Teresa." *My own personal assistant?* I was already falling in love with the job, and I hadn't even started yet.

She made a quick call and then focused back on me. "If you need anything, don't hesitate to ask. I've been here almost as long as Mr. Dorsey himself." She gave me a motherly squeeze. "Welcome to Mystique."

A petite brunette in a pink-checkered blouse with glasses perched on her head pushed open the frosted door and peeked out. "You must be Ms. Romano."

I smiled at the formality. "I am, and it's Gia. Ms. Romano sounds like my mother. You must be Penny."

She did a quirky little curtsy. "At your service. I'm your very own Mary Poppins. Whatever you need done, I can make it happen."

I giggled at her enthusiasm. "Let's start with finding my office and a hot cup of coffee." I turned and gave Teresa a little wave. "Thank you for making me feel welcome."

She pointed at me. "Don't forget... anything you need."

I gave her a thumbs-up and followed Penny into the inner workings of Mystique. Several offices lined both sides of the long hallway. She talked a mile a minute explaining who was who and what was what, finally opening a door about halfway down. "This is your office," Penny said, switching on the light.

It was tastefully decorated with the same black and silver as the front lobby, but empty except for the large wooden desk and a few chairs. The room wasn't big, but it was mine. I ran my hand along the top of the desk, wandered toward the window, and opened the blinds. Hoping to get a glimpse of the Vegas Strip, I was disappointed. All I saw was a loading dock and half a dozen trucks lined up for deliveries.

Penny rushed forward and closed the blinds. "I know. The view sucks. How about I get you that coffee?"

I forced a smile. "That would be great." I reached into my bag, pulled out my favorite pink mug, and handed it to her. "My way of helping the environment. Every little bit counts, right?"

"Right." She held up the mug and read the inscription. *A woman's success isn't measured by the size of her feet.* "Oh, I like you already. I'll be back in a jiffy and then I'll get you up to speed. Cream or sugar?"

Penny's words ran together in a long stream, and I wondered how many cups of coffee she had already drunk. My new assistant was a lot to take in, but I liked her immediately. "A little of both, please."

She disappeared out the door and I slid into the chair behind the desk. The soft leather felt like satin beneath my bare legs. *Only the best indeed.* The office needed a personal touch, and I made a note to do a little online retail therapy tonight. With the money I was saving on an apartment, I could afford a splurge.

I removed the pink executive portfolio and pen set my parents bought me as a going-away gift from my bag and set them on the corner of the desk. With the push of a button, my computer turned on, requesting a password. My lips scrunched to the side. I typed *Mystique* and immediately got an "access denied" message. I leaned on the desk and tapped my fingers against my lips.

Penny rushed in with two cups of coffee and set mine on the desk. Then she dragged a chair around and plopped down next to me. After a long sip from her own cup, she said, "I set your password."

My fingers perched on the keyboard. "And it is?"

"Sassy unicorn ninety-five. Capital *S*, capital *U*."

I lifted an eyebrow. "For real?"

Penny visibly shrank back into her chair. "You can change it."

"I like it." I chuckled. "It's got spunk." I typed the ridiculous password, *SassyUnicorn95*, and my desktop came to life.

"I took the liberty of setting up your email and calendar, as well as organizing your files." She reached for the keyboard. "May I?"

I turned it toward her. "Have at it."

Penny's fingers flew across the keys at an alarming pace, showing me where everything was and the organizational system she'd created for the events. It was overwhelming, but one thing was clear… having Penny on my team was going to be helpful. Everything was color coded and alphabetized.

"We have a floral convention this weekend." She clicked into the file. "Everything is set. We just need to do follow-ups with the catering staff and presenters."

After her overview of the event, Penny opened my calendar. "Shit!"

"What?"

"There's a meeting in the conference room in fifteen minutes. It must have just been added. It wasn't there this morning, I swear."

I put my hand on her arm. "It's fine. No worries." I pulled the keyboard back in front of me. "I have one question for you, Penny. You seem really great at this. When this position opened, why didn't you apply for it yourself?"

Her eyes went wide, and she huffed out a breath. "Honestly, Mr. Dorsey scares the living crap out of me. I'm content fading into the background."

"Penny," I scolded. "No woman should be made to feel like a wallflower. Don't let any man intimidate you. You're better than that." He seemed perfectly pleasant during my interview. Fatherly even.

How bad could he be?

Chapter 2
Trent

I felt like a twelve-year-old child again, summoned to my father's office for some unknown offense I'd committed. As I sat across from his desk, I wondered what the hell I did this time.

"As you know, I had to hire a new event coordinator after your fling with Suzette. Finding someone to replace her on such short notice wasn't an easy task."

So that's what this was about. Again. Suzette with the firm, round ass and voluptuous tits. It wasn't my fault she got attached. She was mediocre at her job, so it wasn't that big of a loss if you asked me.

"She's the third employee you've run off in a year, Trent, and it's wearing on me. If you sleep with one more woman in this office, you won't like the consequences."

I rolled my eyes. I'd heard that threat before, and that's all it was... a threat. "Point made. I'll assume by your need to throw my indiscretions in my face that our new event coordinator is a woman."

My father steepled his fingers. "She is, and Ms. Romano came highly recommended from one of our other hotels."

"Where is she from?"

"Waukegan."

I shook my head. Surely, I couldn't have heard correctly. Las Vegas wasn't for the faint of heart. I expected him to say Miami, LA, or even New York. Certainly not some place I could barely pronounce. "I'm sorry. Where?"

"Waukegan. It's north of Chicago. She worked at the Onyx."

"Chicago is great and all. It's a cool place to hang out, but it's not Vegas. What makes you think she's qualified? I'm fairly certain event planning in Waukegan isn't to the same standards."

I was pushing my father's patience and his lips pressed together in a fine line. "Her job was at one of our hotels. I have faith in my decision. I've been running this business since before you were born. Surely, you're not questioning my judgment."

I knew when to back off. "Of course not. You're the boss."

"You'd be best to remember that. I expect you to help Ms. Romano get assimilated. As COO and Head of PR and Marketing, her success ultimately falls on your shoulders. If you want to take over this empire someday, you'll keep your dick in your pants. It's always been the plan for you to run this company, but I don't have a problem handing over the reins to Hunter if you're a liability."

I cringed. There was no way I was letting my little brother snatch this company from me. He was a wiz with numbers, but it took more than a finance degree to run a prestigious hotel conglomerate. "Message received."

He stood and buttoned his suit coat. "I hope so. I'm serious, Trent. Don't fuck her."

I stood and faced him, buttoning my coat as well. "I won't." There was no way I was screwing up my future and certainly not with some Midwest, corn-fed wannabe.

"Good. I'll expect you to be on your best behavior." He walked to the door, and I followed behind. "Meeting in the conference room in five."

I headed back to my office and barked at my PA. "Tom, coffee. Immediately!"

"Sure thing, Mr. Dorsey." He scurried away to the break room.

The conversation with my father pissed me off. He was going to fire me because I loved women? Please! I hired Tom six months ago. I thought that would help, and it did. I had no desire to fuck him every time he walked into my office. He was also surprisingly good at his job. Efficient and discreet.

Suzette… not so much. We had a fling. That was true. Nothing more than a down-and-dirty fuck to get her out of my system, but it wasn't enough for her. When she showed up in my office wearing only thigh highs and a pearl necklace, it was time for her to go.

I grabbed my portfolio from my desk as Tom rushed into my office with the coffee. "Thank you, Tom."

"Of course. Anything else, sir?"

I sighed. The only place I enjoyed being called sir was in the bedroom. "We've been over this before. It's Mr. Dorsey or Trent. Not sir. And yes, there's one more thing. Find out everything you can about our new event coordinator, Ms. Romano. I wanna know where she lived, her evaluations at the Onyx in Chicago, and any other little interesting tidbits you can dig up." The best defense was always a good offense. Information was power.

"I'll get on it."

"And Tom…"

"Yes?"

"Let's keep this between you and me."

He nodded. "Always."

I made my way to the conference room that overlooked the Strip. It was a glorious sight during the day, but at night it was spectacular. That's when the real magic happened. Any filthy fantasy your mind could conjure up was possible.

Like last Friday night.

The memory of the redhead on her knees in front of Brett and me flashed through my mind. And when we were both deep inside her… pure perfection.

My lips curled into a smile, and I quickly straightened my face. It wasn't the time or place to be reminiscing, especially when my father was up my ass and obviously annoyed.

Business.

I had to prove to him my head was in the game.

Ignoring the rest of the room, I took my seat at the end of the table across from my brother, Hunter. He smirked at me like the cat that ate the canary. "Better pull it together."

"I've got my shit pulled together. Worry about yourself." The last thing I needed was two people up my ass.

He lifted one eyebrow. "We'll see."

My father walked in, commanding everyone's attention, and walked to the head of the table. He threw the pile of papers in his hand onto the polished surface. "I just got the latest numbers. They're good, but they could be better. We're still getting killed by Bellagio, Caesars Palace, and MGM. When people think of Las Vegas, I want Mystique at the top of their list. We need to up our game. We don't need good, we need great."

That was the thing about the hotel industry, especially in Vegas. There was no such thing as status quo. Everyone wanted a bigger piece of the pie. You either kept upping the ante or dropped out of the game. The latter wasn't an option for us.

"I need each department to brainstorm," my father continued his rant. "Everything is on the table from housekeeping to the shopping to the casino to dining and entertainment. Find out what our competition is doing and come up with something better. No idea is off-limits."

I let out a measured breath. Nothing like starting a Monday in a pressure cooker.

My father gathered his papers from the table. "We'll meet back on Friday, but before we go..." He motioned to the other end of the table. "Please welcome our new event coordinator, Ms. Gianna Romano."

My head swiveled that way and her stunning blue eyes locked with mine. The redhead lifted her hand in a dainty wave. "It's Gia. And thank you for having me. I'm excited to be part of this team."

Everyone around the table said their hellos and welcomed her.

My jaw turned to stone. There was no fucking way. God must have really hated me.

Hunter gave me a swift kick under the table as everyone got up to leave. "Good luck."

I scowled at him and pulled out my phone to text Brett.

We have a fucking problem.

Chapter 3
Gia

Fucking fuck, fuckity fuck!

I gathered my things and made a beeline for the door without making further eye contact with Mr. Tall, Dark, and Handsome. What in the world was he doing here?

This was supposed to be my chance for a fresh start.

What happens in Vegas stays in Vegas. What a crock of shit! It was supposed to be my free pass. My one night of erotic exploration.

Now I had to work with him? Hot or not, this situation couldn't be worse. What was I supposed to do? Share coffee in the break room with him like I didn't know about the tattoos on his arms or the monster hiding in his pants.

I plopped down in my chair and buried my head in my hands. What a ginormous clusterfuck. The events of last Friday played over and over in my brain like a porno I couldn't hit pause on, and I was the fucking star.

Oh my god!

He'd seen me naked, and not just naked but completely exposed. The things we did that night... I didn't want to think about it, but now I couldn't stop thinking about it. My panties got wet, and my nipples hardened.

Stop it! Just stop it!

"How was your meeting?"

My head snapped up to see Penny peeking in through the door. I needed to pull it together. *Be professional*, I reminded myself, forcing a smile. "It was good. Mr. Dorsey wants us all to brainstorm ideas to improve the hotel. Maybe after lunch you could give me a tour and fill in some details for me."

"Sure." She stepped into the office, closing the door behind her, and leaned against it. "What did you think of Mr. Dorsey?"

I cocked my head to the side. "He was fine. He definitely knows what he wants, but I have a feeling he's more bark than bite."

She scurried forward and sat across from me. "You didn't find him intimidating?"

I shrugged. "He's my boss. So far, so good."

Penny slapped her palms on her lap. "Great, because he wants to see you in his office."

"Now?"

Her head bobbed and she looked at her watch. "In three minutes to be exact."

My assistant's nervousness made me wary, but regardless of her uneasiness, the man gave me no reason to be apprehensive. "Lead the way," I said, standing from my desk.

I straightened my spine and followed Penny, hoping to exude confidence I didn't quite feel. A pit sat at the bottom of my stomach like a two-ton boulder. I pushed the feeling aside, sure that this meeting was routine. After all, I was a new employee.

My assistant stopped short of an office made of opaque glass and spoke with who I assumed was another PA. "Tom, this is Ms. Romano."

He was a gangly guy wearing a brown sweater-vest and glasses that kept falling down his nose. If he was a day over twenty-one, I'd be shocked. "Hi, Penny," he said enthusiastically, then nodded at me. "Ms. Romano. You can go in; Mr. Dorsey is expecting you."

"Thank you, Tom." *Here goes nothing.* I twisted the knob and entered an enormous office that overlooked the gaming floor. From this vantage point, it was quite the sight to see. The chairback faced me as Mr. Dorsey gazed at his empire. I cleared my throat to let him know I'd arrived. "You wanted to see me?"

The chair spun around with none other than Mr. Tall, Dark, and Handsome sitting there smugly with his elbows on the armrests and his steepled fingers tapping together.

A quiet "*fuck*" left my lips.

"Hello, Ms. Romano."

I didn't know what type of game he was playing, but I wasn't interested in being a timid rabbit waiting for the wolf to pounce. I threw back my shoulders and stood taller. "I was told I was meeting with Mr. Dorsey."

His lips curled up in a wicked grin I wanted to slap off his gorgeous face. "We haven't formally met. I'm Trent Dorsey, Head of Public Relations and Marketing and COO." Waiting a minute for me to digest that information, he added, "Also, your new boss."

A distinct swishing sound filled my ears as all the blood drained from my head. There were two Mr. Dorseys. Penny's words finally made sense. Sure I was going to pass out, I took a deep breath in and let it out slowly. Schooling my face, I sat across from him. "And when did you discover I'd be working here?"

"Are you asking if I knew who you were when Brett and I ate your pussy and fucked your brains out Friday night?"

I cringed. Although his crassness was a turn-on in the bedroom, I found it less appealing now. "That's what I'm asking."

"Not a fucking clue. You were supposed to go home, not show up in my office."

I popped out of the chair and leaned on his desk. "This is my home as of last week. And you approached me, not the other way around."

Trent stood and mirrored my stance. "Obviously, we have a problem."

"It's not a problem for me. Is it a problem for you?"

"Not a damn bit, as long as you don't become a stage-five clinger."

I seethed. "I wouldn't worry about that. Now that I know what an asshole you are, I wouldn't piss on you if you were on fire!" I slapped a hand over my mouth. "Oh, my god." I hadn't even been here a day and I was gonna get canned.

"Sit down, Ms. Romano," Trent said through clenched teeth.

My butt hit the chair.

"Are you done?"

I nodded, still shocked about the words that flew out of my mouth. "Am I fired?"

He sat down and let out a huff. "No. Needless to say, this situation is a surprise to both of us. However, if you can agree to be professional, so can I."

Professional. There was that word again. "Absolutely. I'm sorry about my outburst." The guy might be a jerk, but he was still my boss.

"Apology accepted and appreciated."

That was it. No apology of his own. My teeth clenched together so hard I was afraid I would chip a molar.

"Tell me about your job in Wau-kee-gan," Trent said, stretching the word out like it felt foul in his mouth as he leaned back in his chair.

"I'm from Waukegan, but I worked at the Onyx in Chicago," I corrected.

He waved a hand in the air. "Same thing."

"Not really. While Waukegan is part of the Chicago metropolitan area, it's much more industrialized, with hardworking people not afraid to get their hands dirty. The city of Chicago is more of a hub for finance, commerce, and technology. The cultures of the two cities are vastly different."

The fucker let out a yawn, making a big show of it. "While your geography lesson was fascinating, it didn't answer my question. What did you *do* at the Onyx?"

Trent Dorsey was beyond rude and frustrating. "I was the event coordinator. I planned shit," I gritted out.

"Well, shit is not on the agenda here at Mystique. What kind of *shit* did you plan? You'll have to be a little more specific."

I took a deep breath and sweetened my tone with a smile for the condescending prick. "I planned business conferences, wedding receptions, baby showers, and charity events."

He leaned forward and tapped a pen on his desk. "While we don't have many baby showers at Mystique, the rest I can work with. We also host a variety of shows here: musicians, comedians, Cirque du whatever. Are you going to be comfortable with people like Sarina Lewis and Dale Keyford?"

His attempt to intimidate me fell flat. "This is starting to feel a lot like an interview, *Trent*. Did daddy ask you to do this or are you going rogue?" I stood up. "You know what? If Mr. Dorsey is concerned with my qualifications, I should speak to him myself."

His jaw ticced, assuring me I hit my target as intended. "It's not an interview. I'm just trying to get to know more than your bra size. If my father thinks you're qualified, then I'll have to trust his judgment. Please sit back down."

I did an internal fist pump over the small victory. "Fine. How about you give me a chance and if I screw up, then you can rake me over the coals."

"Fair enough. You'll be reporting directly to me. All ideas and events go through me first. Nothing happens at Mystique I don't know about."

"Understood."

"I'm not trying to be a dick, but if something turns into a public relations nightmare, it falls on me."

I cracked the first true smile since walking into his office. "With great power comes great responsibility," I quoted the famous line from *Spiderman*.

His eyebrows rose. "Cute, but also true. I'm not fucking around, Ms. Romano. If shit goes sideways, someone has to pay the price."

"Is that what happened to your last event coordinator?"

"Not exactly."

I cocked my head to the side. "Then what did happen? Teresa said they left abruptly."

"That's not your concern. What is your concern, is the huge spring fundraiser. We need a charity and an event. The goal this year is five million," he said, spinning a pen around his fingers like a baton.

My eyes bulged. "Dollars?"

"I'm certainly not talking about pesos." The pen stopped spinning and he pointed it at me. "You're not in Waukegan anymore, sweetheart. Welcome to Las Vegas. I want a proposal on my desk by the end of the week. Any questions?"

My head was still swimming. *Five million?* "Not yet."

"One more thing. I emailed you a copy of the employee handbook and highlighted the sections you should pay particular attention to. I highly suggest you read it. You're dismissed," he said as if I were a pesky child who was wasting his time and turned his attention back to his computer.

I guessed that was it. Our meeting was over. I replayed our conversation as I walked to the door. With my hand on the knob, a particular detail stuck out in my mind. "I do have one question."

He raised an eyebrow.

"What's my bra size?"

"Excuse me?"

"You said you knew my bra size, so let's hear it."

Trent's perusal of my body made me feel naked all over again as he scanned me from head to toe. "Thirty-eight double *D*," he said without hesitation. "At first, I thought you were a triple *D*, but you cheated with a padded bra. Anything else?"

I rolled my eyes and left his office, slamming the door behind me. The man was hot as hell and dangerous as the devil himself.

Chapter 4
Trent

Brett lifted his sandwich and took a huge bite. "So, she works with you, huh?" he asked as he chewed, stopping only to catch the pickle that fell down his chin.

I scrunched up my nose. "How do you get so many women? You eat like a pig." My best friend was a bigger chick magnet than me.

"So, sue me. I'm starving. Eating pussy for breakfast doesn't exactly fill you up." He stuffed the last bit of sandwich in his mouth. "Besides, I'm charming as fuck and you've seen my dick. The thing's a python."

I laughed. "Too bad you're ugly."

"Awww. Now you just sound like a jealous little bitch. And you're deflecting." He looked at his Rolex. "I have twenty minutes before I need to get back to work. Tell me about the redhead. Is she as hot in the daylight as she was at night?"

I blew out a breath of frustration. "Unfortunately for me, yes. Her name is Gia Romano and she's a spitfire. Already called me an asshole." I finally took a bite of my own sandwich. With the way my morning went, I was barely hungry. Despite what I told my father, working with Gia was going to be a challenge.

"So, she's got you pegged," he chuckled.

"In her defense, I was a prick to her."

Brett took a sip of his soda and leaned back in his chair, studying me like a fifth-grade science project. "And why is that? You didn't seem to have a problem with her on Friday night."

I shook my head at him and pushed my plate away, having completely lost my appetite. "Don't do that."

"What?" he asked innocently.

"Analyze me. Look for some deeper meaning to shit that isn't there."

"You mean like the fact that you might be interested in this woman?"

I threw my hands up in the air. "I don't even know her. She's from Waukegan. I didn't even know where Waukegan was."

"That's another excuse. You could, I don't know, try to get to know her with her clothes on."

"What could we possibly have in common?"

Brett rested his elbows on the table and held up a finger. "You're both hot."

I chuckled.

Another finger. "You have insane physical chemistry."

That was true.

A third finger. "You work in the same industry. In the same hotel."

"None of that matters. She's completely off-limits, according to my father. Apparently, my inability to keep the party in my pants is wearing on his patience. Suzette was the last straw. Hunter is champing at the bit for me to fuck up." If that happened, I might as well move to Waukegan myself, because there was no way I would stay around to watch him take what was mine.

"You know what I think?"

"Is this going to be a Yoda moment?"

He picked up a french fry from my abandoned plate and threw it at my forehead. "Listen, dickbag. I don't think this has anything to do with your

22

dad. You haven't had a real relationship in forever. I think it has to do with…"

"Don't even say it!" I pushed away from the table and grabbed my phone. "You're crossing a line." I left him to pay the bill and got the fuck out of there.

"It's been five years, man!"

I kept walking.

Five and a half, but who was counting?

When I got back to my office, Tom had a file waiting for me. "Here's the information you requested on Gianna Romano. I got what I could on short notice, but I can keep digging if you want."

"Thank you. I'll let you know." I grabbed the file from his hand and proceeded to my office, ripping my tie off and slamming the door behind me. Falling into my leather chair, I opened the file and took a deep breath. "Let's find out who you really are, Gia."

A copy of her driver's license sat on top of the pile showing her Waukegan address and birth date. She was twenty-seven last month, four years younger than me.

I flipped the page finding a marriage license. My brows furrowed. I specifically asked her about a husband, and she assured me she wasn't married. My finger ran over his name. "Where are you, John Parker?"

I moved to the next page and twisted my lips to the side. She divorced last year. *Interesting.* I sifted through high school yearbook pictures, parking tickets, and college transcripts. Tom, my diligent little lapdog, was thorough in his search.

Three years of work reviews from the Onyx sat at the bottom of the pile.

"Gianna is professional in every sense of the word."

"Gianna Parker is an essential part of our team."

"Gianna's people skills and ability to coordinate successful events have made her indispensable."

The glowing reviews made me wonder why she left a job where she was so valued, until I saw her salary. It was laughable and an embarrassment to the entire hotel industry. Hell, my assistant made more than she did working in Chicago. Gia tripled her salary with the move to Vegas.

I closed the folder with frustration. I didn't know exactly what I was looking for, but none of what Tom found was of any use. There wasn't a single thing that disqualified her from this job. I was stuck with her for the foreseeable future. Eve didn't have shit on Gia in the temptation department. Not only was she beautiful, but apparently that pretty little head was full of brains. A dangerous combination for me and my lack of self-control.

I buzzed Tom and he scurried into my office within seconds. "Was there something wrong with the file, sir?" Seeing my scowl, he amended, "Mr. Dorsey."

"There's nothing wrong with it, it's just not enough. Keep digging. I want the divorce agreement. Search for police reports. Anything she wouldn't want us to know. Find out about the ex-husband, John Parker. I want to know his story too. Scour her social media accounts. If anything looks suspicious or salacious, you bring it to me."

Tom looked up from the notepad he was writing on. "How deep do you want me to go?"

That's what I loved about my assistant, he never asked why. If I said jump, he asked how high. "Use all the resources at your disposal. You have free rein."

He nodded. "Understood. Is there anything else?"

"Have the valet pull my car around. I'm leaving early today."

"Of course." Tom slipped out of my office without further ado. Another quality that made him a perfect assistant was his lack of small talk. There was no *"How was your weekend?"* or any other bullshit I didn't have patience for.

24

I turned and stared out over the casino floor like the king I was meant to be. Nothing was going to stand between me and my empire, especially Miss Gianna Romano.

She had to go.

Chapter 5
Gia

The tour of Mystique took the rest of the morning. Penny was very gracious about showing me every nook and cranny of the hotel and casino. The spa was to die for, so I made myself an appointment for Sunday afternoon. I couldn't think of a better way to celebrate the first week of my new job, and after my meeting with Trent this morning, I was sure I would need a little pampering and relaxation.

My coworkers at Mystique were extremely friendly and welcoming. It didn't hurt having Penny as my guide. She knew everyone by name and the staff seemed to adore her. I'd hit the jackpot with Penny.

Back in my office, she and I unwrapped our sandwiches from the café downstairs. "I didn't want to push, but how was your meeting with Mr. Dorsey?"

I took a very unladylike bite of my sandwich. "Trent?"

Penny nodded.

"He's an asshole, but manageable." I wiped my mouth with the back of my hand. "Don't tell him I said that."

She crossed herself. "Absolutely not. I'd like to keep my job, and besides, I try to avoid him at all costs." She did a dramatic shiver. "I'm pretty sure he could turn me to dust with one look."

I knew exactly what she was talking about, but I also knew the other look he could give. The cocky smirk and sideways smile that melted an unsuspecting woman into a big puddle of mush. I had a feeling I wouldn't be seeing any more of those.

Not that I wanted to.

After our meeting, I pulled up the email he sent me with the employee handbook. As promised, two sections were highlighted in bright yellow... professional attire and the nonfraternization policy between managers and their subordinates. The whole thing pissed me off. First of all, I was dressed totally appropriate. Second of all, the man had an ego the size of Vegas. One night did not equal "stage-five clinger." Yeah, he was extremely attractive and his skills in the bedroom were exquisite, but this was work. I had no intention of mixing business with pleasure. And... he was a jerk with a capital *J*. Trent Dorsey had no problem letting me know I was as insignificant and annoying to him as a mosquito buzzing in his ear. *"Tell me about your job in Wa-kee-gan."* What a condescending prick.

"Hello-o-o." Penny waved her hand in front of me.

I blinked. "Sorry about that."

She pointed to her face in a circular motion. "Your eyebrows are all scrunched up. Do not let that man give you premature wrinkles."

"That obvious, huh?" I sighed.

"I've worked here a while. I'm well aware of the effect he can have on people."

I was sure she was referring to the anger he incited inside me and not the wet spot on my panties. Working with Trent sent me on a roller coaster of emotions. One minute I wanted to stab him with my fancy pen, the next I wanted to relive my Friday night rendezvous. It'd be best to scrub the night from my brain entirely, but I wasn't under any illusion it would happen quickly. The memory of great sex didn't evaporate, especially when I had a constant reminder.

27

Taking my aggression out on my sandwich, I tore another piece off with my teeth and swallowed down the hunk of meat and cheese. "I'm supposed to have a proposal for the spring fundraiser on Trent's desk by Friday. We also need to have ideas to up the quality of the hotel for the staff meeting on Friday. *The* Mr. Dorsey was adamant all departments contribute."

Penny took a bite of her lunch that was much daintier than mine. "We?"

"You and me." I pointed between the two of us. "We."

She slouched back in her chair. "I'm just the assistant."

I abandoned my sandwich and gave Penny my full attention. "You are not *just the assistant*. You know this place inside and out. You have your finger on its pulse. What did you do for your last boss?"

"Suzette? I mostly got her coffee, took notes, and answered phone calls."

Suzette? That was noteworthy. "Then you were underutilized. I don't know much about Mystique, but you do. I would rather we work more as partners. I value your insight and knowledge. What do you think?"

She sat up straighter. "I do have a lot of ideas, but just so you know, I didn't go to college," Penny said sheepishly. "I got this job right out of high school. My dad is friends with Mr. Dorsey. Not Trent. The big guy."

I waved my hand dismissively. "I don't care about a piece of paper. You're more than qualified to have an opinion. Do you have a list of the charities we've supported in the past?"

She raised her finger. "I can do better than that. I have files on every charity event we've run since I've been here, including themes, menus, and entertainment. I've also put everything into a spreadsheet."

I gasped. "Penny, you're a dream come true. Get everything you have and bring your laptop too. I'm going to call Teresa and have a table moved in here. We're going to need room to work."

She hopped up from her seat and headed toward the door. "Do you want coffee?"

I smiled at her. "Actually, I'd love a Diet Coke."

"On it. Anything else?"

My lips pressed together, not sure if I should ask the one thing that'd been niggling at my mind all morning. "What happened to the last event coordinator? Suzette?"

She paused with her hand on the doorknob. "Officially? She got a better offer."

I quirked a brow. "And unofficially?"

Penny held a hand to her mouth as if she were telling a secret. "She had a fling with Trent. Apparently, she got a little stalkerish, so he cut her loose." She made a slashing motion across her throat. "But you didn't hear it from me."

"Hear what?"

She giggled as she opened the door. "I'll be back in a few."

I tapped my nails on the desk. No wonder he was such a jackass this morning. Not only was I a complication he didn't see coming, but he had a history of hanky-panky in the office. It wasn't about me at all. It was about him not being able to keep his sexual appetite under control. Sounded like he was the one who needed to read the handbook, not me.

It was an important piece of information. I had no doubt Trent would fire me without a second thought. I was nothing to him but a random fuck he never expected to see again.

I needed this job. The last thing I wanted was to go crawling back home with my tail between my legs. Regardless of this sticky situation, I was resolved to make it work. If my résumé didn't convince Trent I belonged here, then my performance would. I had to impress him, and something told me he wasn't a man easily impressed.

He might have been determined to see me fail, but I was equally determined to succeed.

Watch out, Trent Dorsey. You ain't seen nothing yet!

The next morning, there was a quick rap on my open door. A handsome, blond-haired man stood in my doorway wearing an impeccable-looking suit. He reminded me of a young Brad Pitt, back when he dated Gwyneth Paltrow in the nineties.

"Come in."

He walked smoothly across my office and stretched out his hand. "I'm Hunter, CFO of Mystique."

I stood and took his hand. "Gia Romano."

He sat down and crossed one leg over the other. "I know who you are, Miss Romano."

Of course he did. I recognized him from the staff meeting yesterday morning. "What brings you to my door this morning?"

"I wanted to introduce myself. See how my big brother was treating you."

"Your brother?"

He straightened his cuff links. "Yes. Trent."

"How many Mr. Dorseys are there?" I asked, sighing. The last thing I needed was another complication.

"Just the two of us," he said with a chuckle. "And my father, of course. I'm the charming one. Trent can be a bit"—he wobbled his head from side to side—"abrasive at times, and I wanted to make sure he was welcoming."

I read between the lines. Hunter was fishing for dirt on his brother, and I wasn't biting that worm. I smiled sweetly. "Rest assured, your brother has been perfectly pleasant. He has an air of professionalism I appreciate. As a matter of fact, I think we're going to work quite well together."

Hunter lifted an eyebrow. "Really?"

"Absolutely. We've already discussed the spring fundraiser and I'll have a proposal on his desk by the end of the week."

He clapped his hands together. "Perfect. If you run into any issues whatsoever, my door is always open. I'm here to help."

It was an odd statement considering Trent made it clear he was my boss. "You mean with the financials for the fundraiser?"

"Absolutely. That or anything else that comes up."

I played along. "That's so sweet of you. You all sure know how to make a girl feel welcome." Charming or not, something about Hunter smelled off. I wasn't sure what it was yet, but when something smelled rotten, it usually was.

"That's what I'm here for. Once you have your proposal finished, maybe we could get a cup of coffee before presenting it to Trent. You know, make sure everything's in order?"

Trent's words rang in my head. *"All ideas and events go through me first. Nothing happens at Mystique I don't know about."* I was sure he wouldn't be happy with his brother's attempt to undermine him.

"That's a very generous offer, Hunter. I'll let you know." I gave him a flirty wink.

His eyes lit up as he stood. "I look forward to it."

Men were so easy to manipulate. At their base nature, they were sexual beings. It might have been unethical to use my feminine wiles on him, but it was certainly effective. "Me too. And again, thank you for checking on me. That was super sweet." I walked around my desk and ushered Hunter to the door. "I'll see you soon."

"For sure," he said, giving me a nod.

I watched him walk away and a shiver ran down my back. I didn't buy his Saint Hunter charade. I was manipulating him, but I had a feeling he was manipulating me too. Something was definitely off.

At least with Trent I knew what I was getting. He didn't make any pretenses. What you saw was what you got.

I stepped back in my office and shut the door.

The Dorsey brothers were double trouble.

Chapter 6
Trent

Hunter walked into my office without knocking. It was an annoying habit, always trying to catch me in a compromising position.

He was wasting his time and effort chasing that rabbit. I'd made a commitment and I intended to keep it. Gia, along with every other woman at Mystique, was off-limits. Vegas was full of beautiful women who didn't work down the hall from me.

"What do you want?" I barked.

My dear brother sauntered over to the window that overlooked the casino and shoved his hands in his pockets. "Just admiring the view. This really is quite spectacular. I'm going to enjoy it."

I chuckled. "You should. It beats the shit out of the view from your office. How do the dumpsters look these days?"

"Laugh it up, big brother. I give it less than a month."

Leaning back in my chair, I gritted my teeth. "Give what less than a month?"

He turned and gave me that ridiculous smile that charmed most people but felt like razor blades down my spine. "Your employment here, of course."

I steepled my fingers casually, tapping them together. "I'm not sure I know what you're talking about."

Hunter propped himself on the edge of my desk. "I introduced myself to Gia today." He let out a low whistle. "She's a saucy little minx... bold and beautiful, with a bangin' bod. And that red hair? I bet she's a wildcat in bed. Probably fucks like a dream."

Yes, she did, but he didn't need to know that.

Since the time he unexpectedly showed up on our doorstep, Hunter always wanted what was mine. I was six the day a blond woman wearing a bright-red miniskirt rang the doorbell. She shoved a duffel bag at my father's chest and handed off the crying toddler she'd dragged up the front steps. "He's yours."

My parents fought a lot over the next few weeks. Days would go by when my mother barely came out of her room. In the blink of an eye, all our lives changed. My father had another son, my mother took in a child who wasn't hers, and I got a brother. Whatever I had, he wanted... my room, my toys, my parents. We were raised as brothers, but we weren't friends. Now he was after my job, my inheritance, and my legacy.

Fuck that!

If he had even an inkling I was interested in Gia, he'd try to take her too. If I couldn't have her, I'd be damned if I'd let Hunter dip his hand in her honeypot. "Tsk, tsk, baby brother. Didn't they cover sexual harassment in your fancy business classes at Stanford?"

"Apparently more than they covered it at UCLA."

"Touché. Although, I never harassed Suzette. She was the one who couldn't stay away from me."

Hunter laughed. "Riiight. I almost think Dad wants to hand this empire over to me, seeing as you can't keep yourself from sleeping with the help. Hiring Gia was genius. She's a walking wet dream."

My jaw clenched. "I know what you're trying to do, but I assure you, I have no interest in Ms. Romano. Our relationship will be strictly professional."

He smacked the edge of my desk. "Glad to hear it. Self-control is the name of the game."

"Is there another reason you're here besides to bust my balls?" He needed to leave before that self-control he talked about snapped in half. I was two seconds from plowing my fist into his pretty-boy face.

"Nope. That's it." He walked toward the door, pausing to adjust his watch. "There is one more thing."

"What's that?"

"I'm meeting Gia Friday morning for coffee. Told her I'd go over the fundraiser proposal before she gives it to her asshole boss."

The hell he was!

At the end of the day, I packed up my shit and headed out. I was still stewing about Hunter's unsolicited visit. He was a cocky little bastard and I meant that in the most literal way possible.

I was ninety-nine percent sure my father's threats were just that…threats. There was no way he'd turn over the reins to his illegitimate son. My mother would never allow it.

My parents loved each other, but lately their marriage was more of a business contract than anything else. They were both hotel heirs. Combining the families was a strategic move made by my grandparents. A way to ensure continued wealth for both sides and build a conglomerate so big, no one could touch it.

Rose Rutherford Dorsey would never agree to her only son being cut from the company. She may not have been involved in the day-to-day operations, but my mother owned fifty-one percent of the company shares and was the head of the board, a fact she didn't hesitate to remind my father of when he tried to exert his power over her.

I smiled despite the warning Hunter issued. The poor boy was delusional, but it didn't mean I was off the hook.

When I passed Gia's office, I peeked inside, then backed up. She was still working. Her red hair was pulled up in a bun and she clenched a pen between her teeth. She looked like a naughty librarian typing away at her computer.

As if she sensed my presence, her head popped up. Gia pulled the pen from her lips. "Hey, Trent. Did you need something?"

"You're still here," I said gruffly. It was after seven and everyone else had left for the day.

She sighed. "Yeah, I know. There's a lot to learn and get caught up on."

I started working here right after college, but I remembered my first week. My father thought it would be cute to put his newly graduated son in the mail room. *"No one starts at the top, son. You start at the bottom and work your way up. It builds character."* What it did was give me an excuse to meet every female employee at Mystique. What can I say? When life hands you lemons, you throw back a shot of vodka and suck the hell out of them.

"You're done for the night. Tomorrow's a new day, Ms. Romano."

She quirked her head to the side. "Is that an order, Mr. Dorsey?"

I pierced her with my eyes. "You'll know when I'm giving you an order."

She attempted to remain professional, but her lips turned up at the corners slightly. "Is that so?"

"I think you know it is." Why was I standing in her office having this ridiculous conversation that was bordering on inappropriate? I should have minded my own business and let her burn the midnight oil if that's what she wanted.

"Yes. I do have a recollection of bossy Trent. He's incorrigible," she said with a straight face.

I shoved a hand in my pocket and leaned casually against the doorframe. "My recollection is that you didn't mind it all that much. Very submissive."

35

All I could think about was Gia on her knees before me. Her hand wrapped around me. My cock down her throat.

Our eyes locked and a beat passed. Then two. She really was beautiful and under any other circumstances, I might be in for a second round with this woman. But the circumstances sucked, and she was prohibited. Round two wasn't even a consideration.

After another beat, she burst out laughing. "That might be the first time in my life I've ever been called submissive."

I repeated her words back to her. "Is that so?"

"Yep." She glanced at the clock on the wall. "Holy cow, I didn't realize it was this late." She began shutting down her computer and gathering her things. "I haven't had much of a chance to explore Vegas. Do you want to get a bite to eat with me?"

I glared at her. My mind was still stuck on the memory of her tits pressed against my thighs. How could she possibly be thinking about food?

She sighed. "I'm not being clingy and it's not a date, Trent. Just two people eating food."

The offer was tempting, but I needed clear boundaries with her. Having dinner together would blur the lines, and twenty-twenty vision was of utmost importance when dealing with Gia Romano. "Can't. I have a date," I lied. *Nice going, Trent.* Of everything that could have come out of my mouth, it was about the dumbest.

Her face fell. "Oh, no biggie."

I drew an uncrossable line in the sand. "Look, we had a good time but that's all it was. A fuck and run. We are not a couple and we're not friends. We're coworkers and I'm your boss. Is that clear?"

The disappointment in her eyes turned to anger. "Crystal." She grabbed her purse and pushed past me. I heard a soft "fuck off" as her shoulder hit mine.

"What was that, Miss Romano?"

She raised a hand in the air as she walked away. "Have a good night, Mr. Dorsey."

I beat my fist against my forehead. That woman brought out the worst in me. But if I wasn't an asshole, I would have bent her over her desk and taken her from behind.

It was better if she hated me.

Chapter 7
Gia

"How's my little sis?"

"I'm good. How's everything at home?" I mindlessly turned the faucet with my toe as I lay in the bubble bath, sipping a glass of cheap wine.

"Hmmm," Bianca mused. "Why do you sound sad? Sin City not what you thought it would be?"

The snarky way she showed her concern was annoying. No one wanted me to take this job. Everyone said I was reaching beyond my class. Trying to be something I wasn't. "Vegas is great. It's everything I wanted. I'm just lonely, you know?"

"What did you expect moving halfway across the country? You can always come home. John would take you back in a heartbeat. You know that man is still crazy in love with you."

I set my phone on the edge of the tub and sank down in the water. "Love wasn't our problem, Bianca. We wanted different things and grew apart."

My sister sighed. "You know I didn't want you to move, but you're there now. You should make the best of it and give it a chance. Get out of that tub and go meet people. Go sit in the bar or something."

I groaned. Sitting in a bar is what got me in this mess in the first place.

"Go on," she continued. "Put on a sexy dress and go meet a hottie. Take advantage of the situation. You know the saying... what happens in Vegas stays in Vegas."

Those were the same words Trent sweet-talked in my ear last Friday. If I never heard them again, it would be too soon. "That's what they say alright. Listen, B, I gotta let you go. My toes are starting to prune up."

"Okay, but I'm serious, G. Get out and enjoy yourself. I'm secretly jealous of you. I'm settled down with three kids and you have the world by the balls. Don't waste it."

We said our goodbyes and I tipped back the rest of my wine. Bianca was right. I didn't want to waste my time in Vegas and trying to be friends with my dickhead boss was a complete waste of time.

I quickly dried off and threw on a pair of cute jeans and a sparkly top. I finished the look with killer heels and released my hair from its tight bun, fluffing it over my shoulders. Inspecting myself in the mirror, I decided it wasn't bad for a quick fix.

My stomach rumbled as I grabbed my purse and headed toward the elevator. The earlier encounter with Trent made me lose my appetite, but now I was famished. Once in the lobby, I browsed my options for food. I wasn't used to eating out alone, but I guessed I should get used to it. When you had moved to a big city that sees twenty thousand tourists a day, the chances of making friends outside the office were slim. My only companion so far was Penny, and it wasn't her responsibility to keep me entertained.

I settled for a casual pub that served burgers and sat down at the bar. One of the upsides of living at a resort hotel was everything I wanted or needed was practically at my fingertips. Want a juicy steak or a slice of pizza? Both were available. Need a pedicure? Make an appointment. Run out of toothpaste? The twenty-four-hour store had you covered. One thing I knew for sure was it wasn't healthy to never leave the grounds. This weekend I was going to get out and about to explore the city.

"What can I get you?" the bartender asked. He was an older gentleman who reminded me of my dad, dressed in a bow tie and vest.

I looked at his nametag. "Hi, Claude. I'm Gia and I started working here on Monday. What's good on the menu?"

He gave me a big smile. "Welcome to Mystique, Miss Gia. Everything is good here, but my personal favorite is the bacon mushroom burger."

"Mmmm. Give me that and a glass of chardonnay."

Claude slapped the bar top. "Coming right up. You want that cooked well done?"

"Medium well," I corrected.

He put the order in and returned with my glass of wine. "So, how are you enjoying your first week?"

I shrugged a shoulder. "It's okay."

"Well, that's not a glowing recommendation."

"The job is fine. I moved here alone and haven't made many friends yet." I shrugged again.

He tapped on his chest with an open palm. "Well, you've got me now. Anytime you want to talk, I'm here."

I held my glass up and saluted him with it. "I appreciate that, Claude. You might get tired of seeing me."

"I doubt that very much," he said with a chuckle. Then he straightened uncomfortably and focused on the man sliding into the chair next to me. "The usual, Mr. Dorsey?"

"Please."

Claude immediately pulled out a rock glass and poured a splash of amber liquid in it.

Hunter took the glass and brought it to his lips. "Stressful day?"

I forced a tight smile. "Not too bad. Just getting a bite to eat since I worked through dinner."

Hunter frowned. "That's not good. Is Trent working you too hard?"

"Not at all. That's all on me." I took a sip of my wine. "I'm trying to get acclimated. I don't want to get fired before I've barely begun."

"I wouldn't worry about that," he said with a wink. "What can I do to help? I'm at your service."

"That's kind of you, but I've got a handle on it. Penny is a godsend."

"Penny?"

How could he not know who Penny was? "Yes, my assistant. She's great. Besides, isn't event planning out of your realm as CFO?"

He rested one elbow on the bar and leaned into me. "I'm a man of many talents, Gia."

I eased back to give myself some personal space. Hunter sent out signals I had no intention of reciprocating and I wondered if he knew what went down between Trent and me. I was saved from responding to his blatant flirting by Claude placing my burger in front of me. "Thank you, Claude. This looks delicious."

Hunter took the hint and threw back the rest of his drink. "I'll leave you to eat. See you tomorrow, Gia."

I took a bite of my burger and gave him a little wave. It might have been rude, but it was better than any words I could think of. Hunter was problematic. He had the same smooth-talking gene as Trent. I fell for it once, it wouldn't happen again. Both Dorsey brothers were off my list. Like scratched out with a fat, red Sharpie crossed off.

I wasn't that desperate for friends.

By Thursday, Penny and I had the details of the spring fundraiser worked out. All I needed to do was finish formatting it into a proper proposal.

"It's good," Penny said. "I wish I could afford to attend it."

I frowned. It hadn't occurred to me that Penny wouldn't be able to afford a thousand-dollar-a-plate dinner. Hell, I couldn't afford to go either. Neither one of us would be able to enjoy the party we were planning. "Me too. I'll talk to Trent about getting us tickets. Maybe he has a shred of decency in that black heart of his."

She sighed. "Let's worry about getting it approved first."

I tapped on the papers in front of me. "What's not to like? It's classy, fun, and for a deserving charity."

"That it is." She held up her hand for me to high-five. "We did great."

I slapped her waiting hand. "We did more than that. We kicked ass."

A sharp knock on the open door interrupted our celebration. "You have some packages, Miss Romano."

I stood up and giddily clapped my hands together. "I'm so excited. Lean them against the wall over there," I directed the delivery guy.

"What are those?" Penny asked after he left.

"These"—I pulled the brown paper from one of the packages—"are inspiration. A little dose of feminism in a man's world."

"Is this Audrey Hepburn?" She ran her fingers over the canvas.

I nodded. "From *Breakfast at Tiffany's*. Have you ever seen it?"

"No, but looking at this, I feel like I should. What else did you get?"

Peeling back the paper from the other two canvases, I revealed what was underneath.

"No way!"

"Yes way. Marilyn Monroe and Raquel Welch. My whole life, people have doubted me, thought I should settle for less. These pictures remind me it doesn't matter where you come from. You can be wealthy or the daughter of an immigrant or raised in an orphanage and still become something great. You can be gorgeous and successful; you don't have to choose. You get to decide your own destiny. These women remind me to be bold, fierce, and fearless."

Penny held her hands to her chest. "Oh, my god, I think I just came a little bit. That was beautiful."

"Oh, stop!" I playfully smacked her on the shoulder.

She did a little shimmy. "I'm serious. I'm totally inspired."

I laughed. "How about you be inspired to find me some nails and a hammer. I want to hang these up before I leave tonight."

"Sure thing, boss." With a salute, she was off and running.

I loved Penny's quirkiness and wondered if she had a man in her life that appreciated the gem she was. I made a mental note to ask her about it.

We'd worked together almost a week and I didn't know shit about her. No wonder I was terrible at making friends.

I went back to my desk and checked my email. Everything was confirmed for the floral convention this weekend, though I could hardly take the credit. Penny firmed up all the details. All I had to do was show up and make sure everything ran smoothly. Piece of cake.

When Penny returned with a hammer and some small tack nails, it was already after five. "You need help?"

"Nah, I got this. Go home and relax."

She crossed her arms and bit the side of her thumb. "I'm your assistant. I'm supposed to be assisting."

"And you've more than earned your keep this week. Go on, girl. Get out of here."

Once Penny left, I should have dove into the proposal, but I couldn't wait to see the iconic women on my wall. I pulled a chair over, stood on it, and tried to pound the first nail into the wall. It should have gone in easily, but the nail barely scratched the surface. I blew my hair out of my face and held the nail steady. Giving it three hard hits, the nail finally sank into the plaster. *Victory!* I hopped off the chair, lifted Audrey from the floor and hung her on the wall. She was gorgeous. So classy and sophisticated. The second picture went up easier, but the third gave me trouble. I pounded the hammer over and over onto the head of the nail.

"That's destruction of property."

Startled, I dropped the hammer and wobbled in my heels on the chair. A hand landed on my butt and another on my waist to steady me.

"Are you trying to kill yourself?" Trent barked.

I stared down at his hand, which was still firmly planted on my ass. "I was doing fine until you scared the shit out of me."

Trent quickly removed his hand and picked the hammer up from the floor. "You were making all kinds of racket. Where did you even get this?"

I swiped the hammer from his hand. "I have my resources." I gave the partially inserted nail two more whacks, hopped off the chair, and hung my last picture.

My "boss" inspected my handiwork. "Those are not company issued and you've put holes in my wall."

I rolled my eyes. The man was more dramatic than a drag queen. "Your wall? This is my office. You don't own the building."

His lips pursed. "Not yet, but I will. Consider this office a rental. If you want to make alterations, then you need to ask." He motioned to my women of inspiration. "Those were not approved."

My eyebrows shot up to my hairline. Control freak didn't even come close to describing him. "Are you serious?"

He threw his hands in the air. "You put holes in the wall. Who's going to fix that?"

"Oh my god! The nails are smaller than your tiny little—"

"Careful, Miss Romano. You're treading a fine line."

I was. I knew I was, but I couldn't help myself. He turned me into someone I wasn't. Driving me to the edge of insanity and pushing me over. I held my hands up in surrender. "Fine. You win. You want my pictures gone? I'll take them down." Begrudgingly, I removed Marilyn from the wall.

"Leave them up. I'll allow your little display of femininity, but I expect you in my office at eight a.m. sharp with your proposal in hand."

"That doesn't work for me. I have an appointment first thing in the morning." He didn't need to know that appointment was with Hunter, and it was more of a casual breakfast than a meeting. I only agreed because I didn't trust Hunter's intentions and figured it would be better to keep him close.

Trent tapped the face of his fancy-ass watch. "Eight a.m., Miss Romano. Not a minute later."

I sucked in a deep breath and released it slowly. "I'll be there."

"Then I'll see you in the morning." He buttoned his suit jacket and strode from my office while I stood there and fumed. He got my blood boiling and not in a good way.

Before I left tonight, I had to finish the fundraiser proposal. Most of it was already complete, I only had the details to finalize. Knowing Trent, if I didn't have all my *i*'s dotted and *t*'s crossed, he'd reject it on principle to prove I was unfit for this job. Besides our tryst, which wasn't my fault, I

44

couldn't figure out why he hated me so much. Well, maybe hate was too strong of a word, but he definitely didn't like me. Thought I was incapable. A naive, Midwestern girl trying to play in the big leagues.

Just like everyone else in my life, he doubted me.

With every word I typed and fact I checked, I had one mission: To prove to Trent Dorsey he was wrong.

Chapter 8
Trent

"No."

"No?"

I slid the proposal across my desk. "That's what I said."

She pushed it back toward me. "You didn't even read it."

"I don't have to."

Her jaw ticced and I could tell she was on the verge of losing it. "What do you mean you don't have to? How do you even know you won't like it?"

Leaning my elbows on the desk, I rested my chin on my folded hands. "A costume party? That's the best you can come up with? That might be cute in Waukegan, but not in Vegas."

As I expected, she clenched her jaw and narrowed her eyes. It was entertaining watching her try to hold it together when I knew she really wanted to tell me to fuck off. "It's not... a costume party." Each word came out distinctly, as if saying them offended her. "It's a masquerade ball."

"Same thing," I said dismissively.

She gritted her teeth. "It's not the same thing. A costume party is childish…"

"Exactly my point," I interrupted.

"A masquerade ball is classy and sophisticated. It's a good theme. A New Orleans inspired event that's fun and for a good cause."

"What's the cause?"

"If you would have looked at the proposal for more than two seconds, you'd know."

That was true, but I rather enjoyed seeing her get worked up. I rolled my hand, indicating she should get on with it. "What's the cause?"

Gia sighed. "Domestic abuse. There are so many women who are physically and mentally abused with no way out of the bad situation they've found themselves in. They live in fear, hiding it from their friends and family. They hide behind a mask, hence the tagline for the event, *Unmask Domestic Abuse.*"

I threw her a bone. An itty-bitty chicken bone, not a fat, juicy T-bone. "I agree. It's a good cause."

Her shoulders relaxed and the lines in her forehead smoothed out.

"But I'm still not approving it."

And just like that, every muscle in her body constricted again. "Why the…" She took a deep breath, reining in her temper. "Why not?"

Something about seeing her get fired up turned me the fuck on and I couldn't resist pushing her buttons. "Because it's a costume party. We don't do costume parties at Mystique. If it fails, that doesn't only fall on you. It falls on me."

"And if it's a success, it falls on you too. It's fancy masks. Ornate and classy, with satin, beads, and feathers. Not freaking clown masks. You hired me to coordinate events. Let me do my job and quit being a closed-minded, narcissistic, pompous—"

I raised an eyebrow at her. She kept tiptoeing on the line, and it wouldn't be long before she tumbled over it.

"Read the proposal, Trent. You'll see it's more than a costume party. It's a black-tie, sophisticated affair." She stood and walked to the door, leaving the proposal behind

Not many people had the guts to stand up to me. It was admirable and refreshing. I found it ironic that in a world ruled by men, it was a woman who had the biggest balls. A very beautiful and sexy woman, which is why I couldn't let her get away with it. "The answer is still no, Miss Romano."

With a hand propped on her hip, she refused to relent. "The answer is not *no* until you read the damn proposal. If you can give me a solid reason for denial, then we can talk." She pointed a slender finger at me. "Read it!"

The door opened and Brett stepped inside without waiting for an invitation, looking like the shrewd businessman he was.

Gia's eyes bugged out when she saw him. She swan-dived over the professional line and fell face-first into inappropriate territory. "Are you fucking kidding me right now? I am not a toy to be played with! Why would you throw this in my face?" Then she turned and poked Brett in the chest. "Don't you even fucking look at me!"

He took a step back and held his hands up in surrender.

I'd had enough of her display of insubordination. I stood and leaned forward on my desk. "You're dismissed, Miss Romano!"

She gasped. "I'm dismissed? You know what?" She flipped me the middle finger. "You're dismissed!" Gia stormed from my office, slamming the door behind her.

Brett jumped from the loud bang. "Jesus Christ! What the hell did you do?"

I laughed. It started low and traveled up my chest until I was in full-blown hysteria. "That was great."

"Great?" He stared at me like I'd lost all my marbles, and maybe I had. "That was a woman who wanted to see your balls on a platter."

I settled myself and waved him in. "Your timing couldn't have been more perfect. She's sexy when she's mad, isn't she?"

Brett lowered himself into a chair. "That was your idea of flirting?" I nodded. "You're a sick fuck. You know that, Dorsey? What did you do to set the redhead on fire?"

I picked up the stack of papers she left behind. "I denied her fundraiser proposal."

"What's wrong with it?"

I shook my head. "Not a clue. I haven't even read it yet. I was going to deny it no matter what."

He tapped his fingers together. "What are you doing? I know you can be a dick, but this is extreme, even for you."

I sighed. "She's got spunk and she's feisty as hell. It's been a long time since a woman challenged me. I like getting her goat."

"Her goat? I think you got her whole damn herd. How do you plan on dating her when you make her want to stab you? You've got me seriously wondering about your methodology. And your mental stability."

"It's better this way. I need her to hate me. Better yet, I need her to quit. Hunter's been poking around, looking for a chance to get my father to turn his back on me."

"Your father won't turn his back on you."

"He might. He made it clear he's done with my manwhore ways, and honestly, Gia is a distraction I don't need." I threw the pen I'd been spinning between my fingers onto the desk and blew out a ragged breath. "What are you doing here anyway?"

"Seeing if you were still pissed at me."

"I'm not a chick. You pissed me off, but that doesn't mean I'm going to hold it against you."

"Good, because I want to revisit my theory."

I rolled my eyes. "Let's not. I don't need a walk down memory lane."

"You haven't had a single meaningful relationship since Morgan." I cringed at the mention of her name. Brett held up a hand. "Hear me out. She was a professional."

"She was a thief," I spat. The memory of coming home to find my apartment and bank account emptied still stung. "And I'm ninety-nine percent sure her name wasn't even Morgan."

Brett leaned forward. "A *professional* thief. A grifter. That's not on you. She pegged you right from the beginning, worked you over, and hung you out to dry. She got you good. Guarantee you weren't the first guy who fell for her ruse."

I rolled my eyes. "Jeez, that makes me feel so much better. I wasn't the only dumbass she scammed."

"Listen, dipshit, I'm not trying to make you feel better. I'm trying to get you to let it go. Morgan was a cocktail waitress in a strip club. She had red flags all over the place. Her backstory was sketchy as hell, but all you saw was her pretty face and sexy body. Since her, you haven't seriously dated anyone. Every time there's an event, you've got a different cookie-cutter, blond bombshell hanging on your arm."

He wasn't wrong. Morgan was the reason I only did one-night stands. The reason I didn't trust anyone enough to take them home. The reason I kept women at arm's length. She destroyed my faith in the fairer sex. But I didn't want to talk about Morgan. So, I did the only thing I could and acted like a dick. "One question. Are you the kettle or the pot?"

"What's that supposed to mean?"

"I don't see you rushing to buy an engagement ring."

"I've had relationships. I just haven't found the one I want to spend the rest of my life with. In the meantime, I've been sampling all the beautiful women this city has to offer. Stop deflecting. We're talking about you, not me."

"Remind me again. Why are we talking about me?"

Brett stood and buttoned his suit coat. "Keep pretending you don't like her. Let's see how that works for you."

"If she's so great, why don't you date her?" I wanted to pull the words back as soon as they left my lips.

He stroked his clean-shaven chin. "Maybe I will. Show her some Sin City hospitality. Perhaps I should think about settling down after all." Brett poked a thumb over his shoulder. "Her office is down the hall, right?"

Now he was trying to get *my* goat and as much as I hated to admit it, the idea of Brett actually dating Gia did not sit well with me. "Don't even think about it. Drinks later?"

He shrugged. "Why the hell not? The Rabbit Hole at seven?"

It was perfect. The distraction was exactly what I needed.

Chapter 9
Gia

I was still fuming from my meeting with Trent. How dare he tell me "no" without even reading the proposal? The man was infuriating.

Penny poked her head in. "Well?"

I blew out a breath and slumped back in my chair. "He said *no*. Didn't even read the damn thing."

She scurried inside and sat across from me. "What? That plan was perfect. We worked so hard."

"Don't worry. I didn't accept his denial. I will get him to see it's a good plan, but I need a little time to cool down."

Her lips quirked to one side. "How are you going to do that?"

"I have no idea yet, but I'm working on it." I'd be damned if I was going to let all our hard work go to waste. I pushed the proposal aside for now and focused on the next issue. "Has Mystique ever had a resident performer?"

"What do you mean?"

"You know, like other hotels have? Wayne Newton? Celine Dion? Brittany Spears? Someone who has a long-term contract to perform here?"

She shook her head. "I wish. All our shows are for one night only. It's exhausting."

"Perfect." I picked up my portfolio, ready for my next meeting. Hopefully, this one would go better than the morning.

The conference room was already crowded when I arrived. I slipped into a chair halfway down the table and took out my notes. This was a good idea. If I couldn't win Trent's favor, maybe the way to do so was through his father. He's the one who hired me, and he was the one I needed to impress.

Trent and Hunter walked in and took their seats, flanking the head of the table. It was hard to believe they were brothers. They looked nothing alike except for their sharp jawlines and impressive cheekbones. Trent did everything in his power to push me away, while Hunter seemed adamant about pulling me closer. They stared at each other with animosity. Whatever was going on between those two, I wanted nothing to do with it. Truth be told, it didn't break my heart to cancel my breakfast with Hunter. There was something about him that set me on high alert. I just couldn't put my finger on it.

Mr. Dorsey, the big boss, came in with a scowl on his face I'd seen mirrored on Trent's and took his place at the head of the table. "Good afternoon, everyone. It's been a hell of a week, so tell me something good. Any ideas to move us up the ranks are welcome."

We all looked at each other, no one wanting to go first.

Mr. Dorsey pressed his lips together in frustration. "Surely, someone must have an idea to get us out of this holding pattern. Please don't be shy. I'm not going to jump down anyone's throats. We need this. I'm open to anything."

I fingered the edges of my portfolio, mustering up the courage to let my voice be heard among the group of veteran employees.

"Sex toys." An older woman, with her gray hair pulled back tightly in a bun, stood and addressed the group.

Murmurs erupted around the room and Mr. Dorsey's eyes went wide, but he refrained from shutting her down. "Explain."

"As head of housekeeping for the last twenty years, I can tell you that guests in the hotel have a lot of sex. This is where people come to explore the fantasies they might not otherwise have the courage to indulge in. Why not give them a little nudge? Something to remember their time at Mystique. Something to come back for."

My own experience in Vegas confirmed her words. There was no way I would have ever given myself to two men back in Waukegan.

"She's kind of right," the man sitting across from me spoke. "Vegas is Sin City. What happens here…" He shrugged his shoulders.

The woman from housekeeping pointed her finger at him. "That's exactly right. Some people are intimidated by sex shops, but if the things they want are at their disposal, they are more likely to try something new." She pulled a pile of papers from the folder in front of her and started handing them around the table. "This is a luxury sex toy shop out of New York. I've already discussed with them the possibility of putting together special kits for us to offer to our patrons. They would be available in every room…" She held up a finger. "For a surcharge, of course. Think of it as a minibar for sex."

There were giggles and gasps as the brochures made their way around the table. I looked at the one in front of me and swallowed. Cock rings, vibrators, and floggers… oh my! My lady parts clenched as my mind went back to the things Trent and his friend did to me. I sneaked a peek at Trent.

His eyes locked on mine as his finger tapped against his lips. He looked like a hungry tiger ready to pounce. I could have sworn he hated me, but what I saw on his face wasn't hatred. It was desire, burning and barely contained.

Hunter tossed the paper aside. "I think it's gaudy and cheap. We're not a brothel."

The older lady scowled at him. "I assure you, there's nothing cheap about anything in this brochure. Sex is natural. What's wrong with turning up the heat a little and injecting some fun into it?"

Trent cleared his throat. "I agree with Greta. There's nothing cheap about this. I think it's a good idea."

Hunter rolled his eyes. "You would."

53

Mr. Dorsey pounded his fist on the table. "Enough!" He smiled at the older woman. "I like it. It's a great idea, Greta. We'll meet later to firm up the specifics."

She nodded at him. "Thank you, Mr. Dorsey."

He motioned around the table with his arm. "We're off to a good start. What else do we have?"

Another man stood. "I've been working with Tony in technology and we're developing an app."

Mr. Dorsey cocked his head to the side. "Tell me more."

"It's an app guests download on their phones. They can check in remotely before they arrive. The app would give us an estimated time of arrival. Valet service will be ready to handle baggage and key cards. It will be faster and more efficient for our guests. The possibilities are endless. We can program the app for room service, reservations, and booking events. Everything a guest could possibly need will be accessible with the push of a few buttons." He backed away from the table and approached the presentation board. "May I?"

Mr. Dorsey gave him a nod.

The man went on to give a full demonstration of the capabilities of the app. By the end, the entire room was eating out of the palm of his hand.

I didn't have anything as fancy as a brochure or presentation prepared. I didn't expect this meeting to be so formal. I pulled my notes from my portfolio and mentally went through all the key points.

"Anything else?" Mr. Dorsey asked.

I took a deep breath and stood, attracting the attention of both Hunter and Trent, who raised an eyebrow. Yeah... I didn't run this by him for fear he'd shoot it down before I barely got it started. This was going to piss him off, but I didn't care.

"I've been looking over the entertainment you've had for the last couple months, as well as the financials for the events. There's no doubt you've had top-tier performers, but each one comes with their own set of complications and additional costs. I'm suggesting something more steady and streamlined. Something that doesn't have us dealing with dozens of riders and demanding musicians."

Trent crossed his arms, rocked back in his chair, and gave me the evil eye. "You mean something that makes your job easier."

I leaned on the table. "I'm talking about something more profitable. A residency. An exclusive event you can only see at Mystique."

"You have my attention, Ms. Romano," Mr. Dorsey said. "What do you have in mind?"

I stepped over to the presentation board and synced my phone with it. I pushed play on the YouTube video and stood back. "This."

The screen came alive, and music filled the room. The young woman with bright-purple hair danced around the stage, sucking in the audience with her phenomenal vocals and sexy moves. The camera panned across the crowd that was going wild. There wasn't an empty seat in the arena. When the video finished, I turned the screen off.

"Is that Ariel Fox?" someone asked.

"It is. She's fresh, hot, and in high demand. Every concert she's performed has sold out in minutes, and don't get me started on the merchandising. I'm telling you, she's a gold mine. People would come from all over the country to see her. We'd be sold out every night. In addition, we're not dealing with different road crews. It provides stability."

"And you think you can get her to agree?" Trent asked skeptically.

This is where my plan had a few wrinkles. I should have gotten a confirmation before pitching the idea, but I'd been too intent on sticking it to my boss today. "I think there's a good chance."

"A chance?" he quipped.

I rubbed my sweaty palms on my skirt. "A good chance. I have an inside contact, but I didn't want to make promises I couldn't keep without running it by all of you first." That was a lie. I didn't have any inside contacts. I was hoping to sign her with sheer determination alone.

Mr. Dorsey gave me an approving nod. "That was smart. I'm on board. See what you can do."

I sat back down and did an internal fist pump. *Take that, Trent!* Now I actually had to make it happen. If I didn't, I'd be eating crow pie and suffering the humiliation my new boss would rain down on me.

I couldn't let that happen.

Penny pulled me through the crowded club and toward the bar. My head swung from side to side taking it all in. Music pulsed and scantily clad women danced in cages hung from the ceiling. The waitresses wore rabbit ears, tight black corsets, and tiny black shorts with puffy little tails. "What is this place?"

"It's a throwback to the Playboy clubs. When the club went defunct, it was bought by someone else, but they kept the vibe going."

When I accepted Penny's invitation to get drinks, I had no idea it would be this. "You brought me to a strip club?"

"It's not a strip club," she insisted. "It's more of a striptease club. There's some erotic dancing, but all the naughty parts are covered."

Maybe I was a prude, but at twenty-seven, I'd never been to a strip club. *You never had a threesome either, but things are changing.* I supposed they were. It was time to break free of the box I'd put myself in. I wanted to explore the real Vegas and it didn't get much more real than this. There was so much going on, I didn't know where to look.

Penny nabbed two seats at the bar, and I hopped up on the stool next to her. The bartender came over. "What can I get you?" She was a pretty woman with long, dark-red dreadlocks piled up on top of her head, a piercing through her nose, and big, silver hoop earrings. Vividly colored tattoos peeked out from her black corset.

Penny leaned forward to be heard over the loud music. "We're celebrating! Two apple martinis."

"I don't know if we should be celebrating yet," I protested.

"Bullshit! We kicked ass this week. We wrote a killer proposal, and you pitched a great idea at the staff meeting. That deserves a drink."

The bartender set our drinks on the rail and hurried off to the next customer.

"A proposal that hasn't been approved yet and an idea I'm not positive I can pull off. I feel like celebrating is a bit premature."

Penny picked up her glass and slid the other toward me. "It's still an impressive first week. It took Suzette three weeks to even get a meeting with Trent."

"Three weeks?"

She nodded as she drank and held up three fingers.

I had an inkling why I'd gotten a face-to-face meeting on day one, but I didn't plan on sharing that information with my assistant. I held my glass up. "To big plans and hoping they come to fruition."

Penny clinked her half-empty glass with mine. "They will. I have a good feeling about you."

"Let's hope I live up to everyone's expectations." I took a sip of my own martini. "So, tell me more about Penny. Boyfriend?"

She sat tall and shimmied her shoulders. "His name is Fred. He's exceptionally loyal, a complete snuggle bug, has the most gorgeous ginger hair, and likes to lick my ears."

That was more than I needed to know. My nose scrunched up unconsciously.

Penny slapped me on the shoulder. "He's a cat, you idiot."

I threw my head back and laughed. "Oh, thank God! I thought you were into some strange fetish thing. I mean, you did bring me here."

She waved a hand in the air. "This is tame for Vegas. Better get used to it. So, whose heart did you break by coming here?"

I cocked my head to the side. "What do you mean?"

"Don't be so coy." Penny wriggled a finger from my head to my toes. "Look at you. You're gorgeous. Surely you broke a man's heart by moving across the country."

My nose scrunched again. "Sadly, no. I dated my childhood sweetheart on and off through high school and college. Getting married was the next logical step for us. Unfortunately, we had different ideas about our future. He would have liked to see me barefoot and pregnant. I wanted more out of life. I wanted a career. He had a hard time being married to someone who was never home. We divorced a year ago."

She pouted. "I'm sorry. I shouldn't have prodded."

57

"It's fine. We're still good friends." I sucked down the rest of my martini and motioned for the bartender to bring us another round. "Who knows, maybe I'll find a man who isn't turned off by a workaholic, career-driven woman."

Penny spread her arms wide. "The world is your oyster. There's no shortage of successful men in this city."

"What does that even mean, *the world is your oyster*? Seriously, who wants their world to be an oyster?"

"Who cares? You know what I mean. You need to get out of your office more. Meet people."

"Well, you're my only friend, so I hope you have room on your calendar to squeeze me in."

She nudged me with her shoulder. "Give yourself a break. You've been here a week. You'll meet people."

"A busy and stressful week. I came here for adventure, but I can't help wondering if I made a mistake. Maybe I'm not cut out for Vegas. What if I bit off more than I can chew?"

"Stop that! Self-doubt is not attractive on you. You're letting Trent get inside here." She poked me on the temple.

"You're right. I can't let him get in my head. I don't know why, but I let him make me crazy. He's just a man, an arrogant man, but a man, nonetheless. I can handle him." With every word I spoke, my confidence built a bit more. I'd let our tryst cloud my vision, but no more. He might have had the upper hand in the bedroom, but I'd prove to him we were equals in the boardroom.

Penny's eyes bulged. "Now's your chance. Incoming!"

I followed her gaze over my shoulder. The devil himself was heading our direction and he looked dangerously delicious.

Fuck my life!

Chapter 10
Trent

What the hell was she doing here?

It was bad enough I was tortured at work. I didn't need her showing up in my off time too.

"Whatever you're thinking, do not do it!"

Brett and I were tucked into a private, rounded booth with a view of the entire club, including the sassy little minx sitting at the bar. She threw her head back and laughed. My dick swelled without my permission. Clearly, he hadn't gotten the message that Gia Romano was off-limits. My cock was still stuck on the feeling of her tight pussy wrapped around him. Of her soft hair brushing against my chest. Her full tits bouncing as she rode me.

None of that mattered now. I was her boss. The line between us was blurry at best. I should have pretended I didn't notice her sitting at the bar with her assistant, but before I knew it, I was on my feet and heading her way.

Brett grabbed my arm and turned me around. "What's your plan?"

Plan? I didn't have a fucking plan. I was working on pure instinct. "I'm not sure yet."

"You're not sure? You always have a plan."

I brushed his hand off my arm. "Relax. I'm not going to do anything impulsive." The lie rolled off my lips with ease. Truth be told, if Brett hadn't stopped me, one of two things would have happened. I'd have either chewed her ass out or devoured her mouth. It was a fifty-fifty toss-up.

"You were a dick to her today. Try starting with an apology," Brett suggested.

I mulled it over. I wasn't just a dick today. I dragged her over the coals all week. "Fine. I'll apologize." I placed a hand on his shoulder. "I'm a big boy. I don't need an escort."

"Oh, but you do. Your self-control is nonexistent where she's concerned."

I rolled my eyes. "Pleeease. Give me more credit than that. I know how to conduct myself around gorgeous women."

"Women you're never going to see again? Absolutely. One who works with you and seems to push all your buttons? I'm not so sure."

Of course, he was right, but I wasn't going to tell him that. "It'll be completely professional. Scout's honor." I held up two fingers.

Brett sighed. "I know damn well you were never a Boy Scout." He turned me by the shoulders. "Come on. I'll be your wingman."

I chuckled. Just like the good ol' days, except we weren't trying to rope some unsuspecting woman into a threesome. I loosened my tie and cracked my neck as we approached the bar.

With all our dillydallying, we lost the element of surprise. Gia already spotted us and tapped her red nails on the bar. "Well, well, well… look what the cat dragged in. And I see you've brought your sidekick." She was already on fire, and I hadn't even said hello yet.

"Ms. Romano," I said curtly.

She rolled her eyes so hard they were liable to fall out of her head. "Cut the shit, Trent. We're not in the office so you don't have to pretend you respect me. Gia will be fine." Her assistant covered a giggle behind her hand.

Although I wasn't keen on being the butt of her antics, I supposed I deserved it. You reap what you sow, and I'd been planting the seeds of her distrust all week. "Then Gia it is." I turned my attention to the brunette. "Hello, Penny."

Her eyes went wide, and I was sure if she could scurry under the bar she would have. "Mr. Dorsey."

I turned on the charm. "As Gia already pointed out, we're not in the office. You can call me Trent."

Brett nudged me to the side and took Gia's hand. "We haven't officially met. I'm Brett and despite what you may think, our meeting this morning wasn't planned. I'm sorry if you felt ambushed."

Her lips twisted to the side as she contemplated the awkward situation. "Apology accepted. For some reason, I believe you." She jerked her head in my direction. "Him, not so much. To what do I owe the pleasure of your company?"

"Well," Brett said. "Trent wanted to buy you ladies a drink for acting liking a total douchebag this week."

My head snapped to him. "I never said that."

"But it's what you meant." He nudged me.

"Is that so?" Gia asked suspiciously.

"Absolutely," Brett answered. "Trent, why don't you pay their tab while I escort the ladies to our table?"

What the fuck? I didn't know exactly what I had in mind but bringing these two women back to our table definitely wasn't it. I handed my Amex Platinum card to the pretty bartender with dreadlocks and waited impatiently for her to settle the tab. I didn't want to leave Brett alone with Gia for too long. He was yanking my chain about going after her for himself, but what if she got sucked in by his charisma? It wasn't a chance I was willing to take.

The bartender handed back my card with a wink. "Have fun tonight."

How was I supposed to have fun sitting at a table with a woman who turned me the fuck on but was completely off-limits? Why couldn't I have a normal relationship with a woman? *Because you tried that once and she robbed you blind.* One-night stands became my default. They were simple... no strings or expectations beyond multiple orgasms.

Gianna Romano had complicated written all over her. Why couldn't she have gone back to Waukegan? Why couldn't my father have hired a man? Men were significantly less complicated and easier to work with.

Back at our table, I found the women in the center of the booth with Brett sidled up next to Gia. I ground my teeth and slid in next to Penny.

Brett leaned his head on his hand. "So, tell me about your fundraiser proposal."

I was going to kill him!

Gia hiked her thumb over her shoulder at me. "What did he tell you?"

"Nothing. He hasn't read it yet."

She narrowed her eyes at me. "Of course, he hasn't."

"It's on my planner. I'm going to read it," I defended myself.

Penny took a sip of her martini, licking the sugar off the rim. "Sure you are," she murmured.

I never noticed before, but with her hair down and glasses gone, Penny was quite cute. Not a classic beauty, but in a quirky kind of way. She'd been working for the company for a long time, and I'd never so much as said hello to her. She faded into the background like a piece of furniture, but it seemed as if Gia was helping her come out of her shell.

"Give me the CliffsNotes version," Brett prodded.

Gia straightened her back, pushing her tits out. The loose shirt she wore slipped off one shoulder, baring her smooth skin and a hint of the ink I knew was hidden underneath. "It's a New Orleans-themed masquerade ball to benefit domestic abuse. A thousand dollars a plate, a Dixieland jazz band, and a silent auction."

"Don't forget the surf and turf," Penny added. "We haven't got the entire menu figured out yet, but steak and seafood definitely. Oh, and a dessert bar to die for."

"You need crawfish and shrimp. My mouth is watering just thinking about it," Brett said.

Penny clapped her hands together. "You know what else we need? A tarot card reader and a fortune-teller. Totally New Orleans."

"Yes, and yes! It all goes together." Gia leaned across Penny and glared at me. "Mystique. Mystery. Masquerade. Masks. It'll be fun and profitable."

"It's a costume party," I refuted. "We don't do costume parties."

Gia waved her hand at me. "That again? You're hopeless. You wouldn't know fun if it bit you in the ass."

"I know what fun is." All three of them were ganging up on me.

"Sign me up." Brett slapped the table. "But you're underselling it. You can easily charge five grand a plate."

"Five grand?" Gia fanned a hand in front of her face. "No one's going to pay that."

"This is Vegas." He spread his arms wide. "People have money and it's for a worthy cause. I can hook you up with names of the A-listers."

"Can you send them to me?" Penny asked. "I've already got a spreadsheet started. With your help, it'll be the Who's Who event of the year." Penny slapped hands with Brett and Gia as they celebrated.

I cleared my throat and undid the top button of my shirt. I wasn't thrilled at how friendly the three of them were acting. Brett was encroaching on my territory. How was I supposed to keep a professional relationship with Gia with all his *sign me up* and *I can hook you up*? He was a terrible wingman. "You're forgetting one thing. I haven't approved the event yet. Maybe you should wait for the green light before you get all crazy."

Gia glared at me. "Riiight. Nothing happens without your approval. I heard you, loud and clear."

"I'll read the proposal this weekend and let you know on Monday." I'd have to stop by the office tomorrow and pick it up. I was planning on making her sweat it out a bit longer, but now that it was three against one, I'd be a total jerk if I made her wait. She raised an eyebrow at me. "I promise."

"All I want you to promise is to keep an open mind. And read it, don't skim it. Penny and I worked our asses off to get that proposal finished by the end of the week as you requested."

The brunette finished off her martini in one gulp. "And on that note, I need to use the ladies' room. Can someone let me out?"

I slid out of the booth, so Penny could leave, then slipped back in closer to Gia. As the waitress came by, I ordered the table another round and rested my arm on the back of the booth behind Gia.

She looked between the both of us, sipping the last of her drink. "Now that Penny's gone, let me be frank. What happened between the three of us was a first for me. It was fun, but it's not happening again."

Brett chuckled. "Believe it or not, this is a first for us too. Not the ménage à trois, but this." He motioned between the three of us. "We've never met up with one of our... how shall I say it?"

"Conquests?" she provided.

I cringed. "That sounds so tawdry."

"Let's not pussyfoot around it. We had an anonymous... now, not so anonymous... threesome. I don't regret it, but it does complicate things. I'm not a cheap whore to be played with. I came to Vegas to start a career. I don't want to be the butt of some joke between you two. I want to be taken seriously."

"You were never a joke to us," Brett said. "You're a beautiful, sophisticated woman. I won't treat you as less."

Seeming satisfied with his answer, she turned to me. "And what about you? Are you going to quit treating me like a pariah that crawled out of the gutter to ruin your life?"

"Pfft! I haven't done that."

She pursed her lips. "Well, you sure as hell haven't rolled out the welcome wagon. You treat me like I'm stupid and not worth your time. How about you give me a chance?"

"So, you want to be friends?"

"You've already made it clear we're not friends, but I don't want to be enemies either. I want a chance to prove myself without being tripped up every day."

What she was asking for was fair. Should have been expected even. If she'd been anyone else, I would have never been so hard on her. "We can try being friends, but I'm not giving you any preferential treatment."

Gia crossed her arms. "I don't want preferential treatment, just an even playing field." The waitress returned with our drinks. Gia reached for her martini and held it up. "To new friends and starting over."

"To new friends," Brett chimed in.

I clinked my glass with theirs, sealing the deal. *Wait! What just happened? I'd friend-zoned myself?* I sighed, knowing it was for the best.

Penny returned when we were midtoast. "What'd I miss?"

Brett tapped the seat next to him. "We're celebrating new friends. And to Trent and Gia not killing each other."

She picked up her fresh drink and clinked it with ours. "I'll drink to that. They've been at each other's throats all week."

"Nice," I mumbled. The hostility between Gia and me was a living, breathing entity that hadn't gone unnoticed. Bringing it down a few notches was in both our best interests. The problem was when I let go of the anger, lust took the reins. I fantasized about bending her over my desk and reminding her how good the sex was between us. But now I'd friend-zoned myself. Seemed no matter what I did, I was fucked.

The lights dimmed and the DJ came over the loudspeaker. "Ladies and gentlemen, I'd like to direct your attention to the main stage for the lovely Laney!" We had an excellent view of the raised platform in the middle of the room.

Gia leaned back into the crook of my arm and whispered, "Is this a strip show?"

I winked at her and smirked. "Nothing so scandalous as that. It's much classier. Relax and enjoy the performance."

She bit her lip, and the club went black. Spotlights twirled around the room and converged in the center of the stage. A woman dressed in a suit stood with her back to us and "You Can Leave Your Hat On" started to play. Her arms gracefully floated out to the sides before resting on top of the black fedora that concealed her hair. She gave a little wiggle of her ass, teasing the audience with her hips. When she turned around, her face was half-hidden by the hat as she strutted to the front of the stage. Grabbing the lapels of her jacket, Laney eased it down her shoulders, then pulled it back tight to her chest. After a few sexy denials, she slid the coat down her arms and flung it to the side. It was an erotic move that elicited wolf whistles around the room.

Next, she played with the suspenders, tugging them with her thumbs and stretching the elastic. In one swift move, she pushed the suspenders and wide-legged trousers down her hips, where they fell into a heap at her feet. With a single step and flick of her leg, she effortlessly kicked the pants away.

Laney pranced around the stage in heels and stockings, letting the shirt sway around her thighs as she removed the red tie, seductively swinging it around her body and dragging it across her breasts. Half dressed, she managed to be more alluring than most strippers I'd seen who knew how to work a pole but not an audience. Laney was a trained dancer, taking her clothes off was secondary.

I glanced down at Gia. Her tongue ran along her bottom lip, and I had the urge to lick it. I let my arm dangle down until my fingers brushed the soft skin of her shoulder. She looked up at me with her big, blue eyes and blinked as her breath hitched. From this vantage point, I had a good view of her abundant cleavage, and I didn't hide the fact that I was sneaking a peek. Her nipples hardened, pushing the thin material of her shirt into perfect points. She wiggled on the seat next to me. I knew the signs… she was turned on. From me or the naughty show, I wasn't sure. I was guessing both. "Watch the stage, Gia."

As if she hadn't realized her eyes were locked on mine, she quickly adverted her gaze to Laney. The dancer slowly undid the buttons of her shirt, deliberately keeping what was underneath hidden. She teased the material off one shoulder, then the other, careful not to reveal too much. When the music hit a crescendo, she ripped open the shirt and shimmied her shoulders before letting it slide down her arms and drop to the floor.

The dancer had the entire crowd, both men and women, mesmerized. She pulled the strap of her bra, easing it down and back up. Then she wagged a finger at the audience in a nuh-uh gesture.

The guys at the next table groaned. I felt their pain. My dick was incredibly hard, but it had nothing to do with the woman on the stage and everything to do with the redheaded temptress sitting next to me. It was pure torture.

I focused back on Laney. The hat finally came off and long, dark locks spilled down her back. She whipped her hair around and ran one hand through it as she flung the fedora into the crowd. It landed in a guy's lap and his friends cheered wildly. Laney blew him a kiss and strutted off the stage as the music ended.

"Give it up for the very lovely Laney!" The lights came up and the room filled with thunderous applause. "That's how we do it here at The Rabbit Hole! Don't you go anywhere. The night has just begun." The DJ pumped dance music through the speakers, bringing back the club atmosphere.

Gia scooted away from me and leaned toward Penny. "That was amazing!" she yelled over the music.

Penny clapped her hands excitedly. "I knew you would like it. I'm so glad we came."

"Unfortunately, I need to call it a night or I'm going to turn into a pumpkin." Gia finished her drink and set the glass in the middle of the table.

I looked at my watch. "It's barely nine o'clock."

Her lips twitched to the side. "Some of us have to work tomorrow." I looked at her blankly, and she shook her head. "The big floral convention? The event coordinator," she tapped her chest, "needs to make sure everything runs smoothly."

I forgot all about the convention Suzette set up before she left. Damn, where was my mind? "Of course."

"I should get home too," Penny said. "Fred will be wondering where the hell I've been all night. He gets hangry when his dinner is late." She slid out of the booth and grabbed her purse.

"Sounds like you need a better boyfriend," Brett said, echoing my thoughts.

The brunette blushed. "Oh, I don't have a boyfriend. Fred is my cat."

Brett smirked. "Good to know." I could swear he was flirting with her, though she wasn't his usual type.

"Do you ladies need a ride home?" I asked as I let a tipsy Gia out of the booth. I was bummed our night was ending early, even if it was irrational. I couldn't remember the last time I had fun with a woman outside of the bedroom.

"That would be—" Penny started.

Gia grabbed her arm. "We'll take an Uber home. Thank you for the drinks. It was nice to officially meet you, Brett." She barely acknowledged me as she dragged her assistant away.

Penny stumbled and gave us a wave over her shoulder. "Thank you!"

"You're welcome!" Brett yelled.

I scowled at him.

"What?"

"You're not fucking her, that's what. Penny isn't even your type."

He leaned back in the booth and swirled the ice in his almost empty glass. "Says who?"

"Every woman you've ever dated before."

My best friend shrugged. "Maybe I'm ready for something different. She's smart and witty. I like a woman with a brain."

I laughed. "Since when?"

"Don't bust my balls. Besides, you have your own love life to worry about. I'm wondering how you're going to work with Gia and keep it platonic. You could practically feel the sexual tension rolling off the two of you."

"I have no fucking idea."

Chapter 11
Gia

A shrill ring pulled me out of a deep sleep. My hand blindly groped the nightstand for my phone. I wrapped my fingers around the device and pulled it to my face. Even with my eyes half-closed, I could see the screen was black, yet the ringing continued.

With every reverberation, it felt like someone was poking me in the brain with a knitting needle. I shouldn't have had that third martini last night, but I got caught up in the atmosphere and threw caution to the wind. It was stupid on so many levels.

I grabbed the receiver from the room phone and brought it to my ear. "Hello," I grumbled.

"Ms. Romano, I'm sorry to bother you so early. I have a Debra Stanton on the phone for you. Something about the flower convention today."

I searched the foggy recesses of my brain. *Debra Stanton? Who the hell was she?* Finally, it came to me. "Oh, our keynote speaker. You can put her through."

"One moment."

I waited patiently for the call to be transferred. As soon as it was, loud coughing and sniffling came through the line. I pulled the phone away from my ear. "Hello?"

Another cough. "Ms. Romano, this is Debra Stanton." Sniff, sniff, cough. "I'm not going to be able to attend the convention." Then there was the unmistakable sound of retching and a flush. "I'm so sorry, I think I have the flu."

That wasn't what I wanted to hear at seven in the morning the day of the event, but the woman was clearly ill. Getting upset with her wouldn't be helpful. "I'm so sorry to hear that. Don't you worry, we'll figure it out."

The sound of retching came through the phone again. "Thank you. I really feel terrible."

"No worries. Please take care of yourself, and I hope you feel better." I hung up the phone before being subjected to another round of vomiting.

Well, that was a rude awakening. It was time to get up anyway, but now I had a major problem to solve in a matter of a few hours. No keynote speaker was a huge issue. I started the coffee maker, jumped in the shower, and got myself ready for the day. *Where the hell was I going to find a keynote speaker on such short notice?*

There was only one option, and it was a Hail Mary at best, but I was desperate. Grabbing my coffee, I took the elevator down to the main lobby and started toward the shops. Some were open twenty-four hours, but the one I needed didn't open until nine. I stood in front of the glass doors and pressed my face to the window. It was dark inside, but a glow came from the back of the shop. I pounded my fist against the glass and teetered in my heels from side to side, hoping someone was there. After a minute passed, I tried again.

Finally, a tiny woman in her early fifties came to the door, turned the lock, and poked her head out. "We don't open for another hour," she said in her thick French accent.

I sighed a breath of relief. "Genevieve."

She narrowed her eyes, then they widened in recognition. "Gia?"

"Yes, we met the other day. I really need your help." Thank goodness for Penny and her tour or I wouldn't have even known we had an in-house florist.

Genevieve opened the door wider and beckoned me in. The scent of roses, lilies, and lavender was almost too much in the small space. "What can I do for you?"

"As you know, the floral convention starts today."

The lines in her forehead deepened. "I'm aware. I'm putting the finishing touches on the arrangements." She moved into the back room, and I followed.

Scattered around the space were dozens of floral arrangements, each one unique and more beautiful than the last. I raised my hands to my mouth. "Oh, Genevieve, they're gorgeous!"

She laughed. "You doubted me, *mon chéri*?"

I shook my head. "Not for a minute, but I have a problem. The keynote speaker canceled on me. She's sick as a dog."

"*Merde!* That is a problem. What are you going to do?"

"Well, I do have an idea." I tapped a fingernail against my lower lip. "Remember the story you told me when we first met? About how you grew up in Paris and your mother owned a floral shop along the Seine?"

"But, of course. I spent every day of my youth in that shop."

I smiled. "And how you told me you didn't choose the flowers, the flowers chose you? How they whispered to you?"

Genevieve laughed. "I know it sounds silly, but it's true."

I shook my head. "It's not silly at all. It's perfect. How would you like to be our keynote speaker?"

She gasped. "Me? I don't know anything about public speaking. I'm just a florist."

"And a florist is exactly what I need. Tell your story… about growing up in France, working at your mother's shop, coming to America, and how the flowers speak to you. You can use these arrangements as props and explain what inspired your designs. Maybe answer a few questions from the audience. You're charming. Just be you."

71

I could see her wheels turning as she considered my proposition. "I don't know."

My hands came together in front of my chest in a praying position. If she didn't agree, I was totally screwed. It would be one more thing for Trent to hold over my head. "I'll pay you double what the other woman was getting." It was a generous offer and likely one I'd have to pay out of my own pocket.

Genevieve gasped. "*Mon dieu!* I'll do it, but only because it was you who asked, and I don't want to see you sink in your first week. I like you, Gia." She reached up and pinched my cheek. "*Vous avez du cran.*"

I looked at her blankly. "I don't know what that means."

"It means you've got guts. Spunk. I admire a woman willing to take chances."

I hoped Trent felt the same way.

"Bonjour!"

I stood at the back of the conference room and snapped pictures as Genevieve took the stage. I was afraid our audience might be upset with the unplanned change, but within minutes she had them eating out of the palm of her hand. Her passion for flowers flowed through the room like a melody that soothed your soul. She was both captivating and inspiring.

"Why is Genevieve on the stage?"

Trent's deep voice in my ear startled me. He raised an eyebrow, waiting on my response.

"Our keynote speaker canceled this morning," I whispered. "I was desperate, so I begged her to fill in." I raised my hand to stop his impending rebuttal. "I know I didn't get this approved by you, but it was an emergency, and I didn't have your cell number. I made a decision, and you'll have to deal with it." The smell of his cologne made my chest flutter with unwanted desire. My body clearly hadn't got the memo that Trent Dorsey was my boss and a second round between the sheets was never happening. Besides, he was a jerk. A hot jerk, but still a jerk.

"I see," he said, leaning against the wall. My body tensed as I waited for the reprimand that was sure to come, but he just listened as Genevieve explained how the flowers spoke to her. "She's good. Suzette should have hired her in the first place."

That alleviated some of the stress, but I had another bomb to drop on him. "I'm glad you feel that way because I promised her double what we were paying the original speaker. Like I said, I was desperate."

He cringed. "We'll make it work. She's worth every penny for saving our asses."

His words were a relief to me and my wallet. "Thank you."

"For what?"

"Not chewing me out. I expected you to be pissed." I crossed my arms defensively.

He pushed off the wall and crowded my personal space. "Despite what you may think, I'm not unreasonable. I appreciate your quick thinking and ability to resolve what could have been an embarrassing situation for the hotel. Good work."

As Trent turned to leave, I tugged at the sleeve of his suit coat. "Did you read my proposal yet?"

He tapped the rolled-up papers in his fist. "Got it right here. We can discuss it on Monday. Good luck with the rest of the convention, Gia."

Gia.

That was the first time he'd used my first name at work. We were making headway. *Maybe going to The Rabbit Hole last night wasn't a mistake after all.*

Chapter 12
Trent

I walked in on Monday to find an unwanted visitor in my office. "Can I help you?"

Hunter put the picture in his hand back on the shelf and carefully adjusted it. "What? I can't stop in to see my big brother?"

"What do you want, Hunter?" I tossed the fundraiser proposal on my desk and booted up my computer.

He strode to the window, hands in pockets, and gazed down at the casino floor. "Just checking what the view will be like when I take over your position. I stopped in to see Gia this morning."

My patience for Hunter was thin on a good day, but when it came to him talking about Gia, I had none. "And?"

He turned his attention to me. "Her ass looks phenomenal in that tight black skirt. And don't even get me talking about her tits. That woman was built for sin. Gets my dick hard every time I see her."

My temperature rose, but I kept my cool. A reaction was exactly what he wanted. "Careful. Sexual harassment is real."

"You would know."

"There's a difference between harassment and consent. Clearly, you don't know the difference."

"I'm not the one being held under a microscope."

He was giving me a migraine. The back-and-forth was senseless. "Is there something you needed?"

"Nope. I got what I came for."

"Then you won't mind seeing yourself out. Some of us have work to do."

He dragged himself away from the casino window and headed toward the door. "Sexual frustration makes you testy. You should do something about that."

What a prick.

I buzzed Tom. Not even five seconds later he stood before my desk, notebook ready. "Sir? I mean... Mr. Dorsey."

The kid was as uptight as a whore in church. "Relax, Tom. Have a seat." He straightened his bow tie and carefully eased into the chair. "What have you found out about Miss Romano?"

Tom flipped through his notes. "Nothing. She's clean as a whistle. Even paid all her parking tickets."

"Hmmm. And the ex-husband?"

"Works in a factory. Looks like she filed for the divorce, citing irreconcilable differences. However, according to her social media, they're still friends." He pushed his glasses up his nose. "You want me to keep digging?"

I shook my head. "Nah. I've got what I need. Could you call her in here please?"

"Sure thing." He popped out of the chair and was gone in a flash. The kid needed a good dose of Xanax.

I smoothed out the rolled papers on my desk. Reading a work proposal on a Saturday night wasn't exactly my idea of fun, but I was pleasantly surprised to find it well written and detailed.

The door creaked open, and Gia poked her head in. "You wanted to see me?"

I held up the papers. "I read it."

She stepped inside and closed the door behind her. Hunter wasn't lying. Although her clothes were completely professional and covered plenty of skin, her curves were clear as day, and she looked sexy without even trying. "What's your decision? Are we going to be making the ballroom into the French Quarter?"

I chuckled. Gia was darn adorable when she wasn't trying to rip my throat out. "It's a possibility."

She cocked her hip and rested a hand on it, twisting her lips to the side. "Trent…"

"It's approved," I said before she went on another tirade.

"Oh, thank goodness." Gia made her way forward and sat down, her skirt riding up her long legs.

"You can thank Penny and Brett. If the three of you hadn't ganged up on me, I probably wouldn't have read it until today." I spun my pen around my fingers to keep myself centered.

She giggled. "I would say I'm sorry, but I'm really not. At least one good thing came out of the night."

My eyes locked with hers. "I'd say more than one. Hopefully, our rocky start is behind us, and we can move forward with a little less hostility." Her eyes narrowed into slits. "From both of us," I amended.

Gia waved her hand in the air. "Of course, we're friends now."

I cringed. *Stupid friend-zone.* With Hunter snooping around, it was better. I didn't need to give him any ammunition. "Are we? Or was that the alcohol talking?"

"I never wanted to be your enemy, Trent. The way we met was… unconventional… but it doesn't change the fact I came here to do a job." She fidgeted with some loose hairs and tucked them back into her updo. "It was a surprise, is all."

I chuckled. "For both of us, I assure you." I couldn't take my eyes off her. Memories of having her under my tongue and the soft little whimpers she made flooded my mind.

She cleared her throat and motioned to the papers on my desk. "So… the proposal."

Right. "It was well thought out and thorough. I can tell you put a lot of work into it."

"Penny helped. She's way undervalued here. Actually, she probably should have been offered this position instead of me."

"Be that as it may, I think my father hired the right person." I picked up the papers and scanned the notes I'd made in the margins. "I have some thoughts on this, and I'd like to go over the specifics with you, but I'm in back-to-back meetings until four. I was thinking I'd order us carryout and we could discuss it over dinner."

Gia's eyebrows rose up to her hairline. "I thought we weren't allowed to eat together. You made that pretty clear last week."

"I'm sure we can both agree I was being an asshole."

Her lips curled up. "Your words, not mine."

"I can admit when I'm wrong. Any requests for dinner?"

She tapped a painted nail against her lips. "Is there a good Thai place in town?"

Her choice surprised me. I doubted they had many Thai restaurants in Waukegan. "It's Vegas. We have everything. Anything specific?"

"Pad Thai with shrimp, medium hot."

"You like it spicy, huh?" The words slipped out with a chuckle before I could stop them.

"I think you already knew that. See you at four." She gave me a wink and strutted from my office, giving me a fantastic view of her long legs and round ass.

Ugh! Down, boy.

"How's Gia working out?" my father asked without looking away from his computer.

If he was so interested, you'd think he'd at least give me the courtesy of eye contact. "It's fine."

He leaned back in his chair and momentarily closed his eyes. "Fine is the kind of answer your mother gives me when things are *not* fine. Is there an issue?"

"Absolutely none. You were right about her; she's smart and organized."

"And how are you two getting along?"

I wobbled my head back and forth. "It's a work in progress, but it's moving in the right direction."

"I see. Anything else I should know about?"

"Not a thing. Since she started working here, everything has been completely professional." It was a stretch at best, but what the hell else was I going to say?

"Good to hear." My father pulled on his tie and loosened it. "I wanted to let you know that I'm going to be out of the office. Your mother and I are doing a cross-country tour of our other hotels to check in and make sure everything is running as it should."

"Wow! You two haven't done that in years."

"I know. It's long overdue. It's not much of a vacation, but we're going to try to sneak in some fun too."

I couldn't remember the last time my parents went on a vacation together. Their marriage wasn't awful, but since Hunter showed up, it was more of a business arrangement. "You hitting the hotel in Honolulu?"

"It's actually our first stop. Your mother insisted. She wants to lie on the beach for a few days before we start scoping out the other hotels."

I laughed. "You're going to relax?"

"I'm going to try." He leaned forward, resting both arms on his desk. "While I'm away, you're in charge. Consider it a test run."

"Don't worry. I can handle it. How long will you be gone?"

"A while. We'll be back right before the fundraiser. Your mother doesn't want to miss Gia's big event."

That struck me as strange. "Does Mom know Gia?"

"Who do you think vetted all the applicants? Gia was her top choice. After I interviewed her, I could see why."

I thought my mother had taken a back seat, but apparently, she was more involved than I realized. "So, when are you leaving for your trip?"

"Thursday. Airfare is cheaper during the week."

I shook my head and chuckled. Our family could afford a private jet if we wanted, but my father wouldn't hear of it. "You don't need to worry about money, Dad."

"Just because you have money doesn't mean you should waste it." He gave me a wink. "It never hurts to save a penny where you can. My father taught me that."

Although it was true, it sounded ridiculous coming from a man who was a multimillionaire. My dad was selectively frugal. I never had to worry about money while growing up, but nothing was ever handed to me. He made me work for it and I was a better man because of it.

The last thing I wanted to do was disappoint him.

Chapter 13
Gia

I grabbed my laptop and the folder containing all my notes for the fundraiser and headed to Trent's office. He shocked me by suggesting a working dinner. Mr. We're-not-a-couple-and-we're-not-friends had no problem putting me in my place last week. It was nice to see him loosening up. Weird, but nice. I'd gotten used to his gruff demeanor and wondered if this was some type of sick trick he was pulling. Luring me in with Thai food, then snaring me in a twisted trap. I may not have wanted to strangle him this morning, but I wasn't even close to trusting him.

The door was cracked when I arrived. Trent sat at a round table with his laptop open. He stared at the screen while spinning a pen in his fingers.

"Knock, knock."

He tossed the pen down. "Come in. I thought we'd work at the table instead. More room to spread out."

I dropped my things on the table and walked toward the tinted window. The few times I'd been in Trent's office, I was too distracted to look. I placed my hand on the window and gazed down at the casino floor. You could see everything from up here. Four o'clock on a Monday and the place was alive and bustling. "It really is like magic."

"What is?"

"The casino. Before moving here, I'd never been to one."

Trent came and stood next to me, hands in his pockets. "Really? They don't have casinos in Illinois?"

I pressed my face closer to the window. "They do, but I didn't have the time or money to enjoy them."

"So, you've never pulled the handle on a one-armed bandit?" he asked in amazement.

"Nope. I never understood the draw."

"What about poker?"

"I know how to play poker, but we used to play for dimes when I was in college. Nothing like this." I motioned to the scene below.

"Hmmm. Our stakes are a bit higher than that. Our high rollers can easily spend ten grand a night."

My head spun around. "Are you serious? Ten thousand dollars in one night?"

"Sometimes more." He went back to where our work was laid out. "That's not the norm though. Our lowest table is fifteen bucks if you want to give it a try."

I headed to the table and opened my laptop. "Seems like a waste of money. I can think of better things to spend it on." While growing up, finances were tight. We didn't have money to spend on frivolous stuff. The only reason I was able to go to University of Chicago was because I got a scholarship. My parents still didn't want me to go, but I couldn't wait to get out of Waukegan.

Living so close to downtown Chicago changed my life. It inspired me to want more for myself. I wanted to live in one of those high-rises one day. I wanted to become somebody. I wanted to be where the action was.

I sat adjacent to Trent and internally cringed when I saw all the notes made on the proposal. "All of that needs fixing?" I wanted to think my work was flawless. Prove I could do the job Mystique hired me for.

"No. They're questions, places it needs more detail, and my own ideas. We'll get to all of it."

I glanced at the clock. "That's a lot. How long is this meeting going to last?"

His eyes narrowed. "As long as it takes. Why? You got a hot date or something?"

I laughed at his absurdity. "Not at all. I have no social life. The only people I know are Penny and Claude."

"Who's Claude?"

Was that a hint of jealousy I detected? "Just a guy I have dinner with every night."

Trent's jaw clenched. "Huh."

So, maybe it was jealousy. I could jerk his chain, but there was really no point. "He's the bartender in the pub downstairs where I have dinner. Claude's like sixty, but he's friendly and somebody to talk to. Better than eating alone."

His shoulders relaxed. "I would think you'd be anxious to get home at the end of the day."

"This is home." I motioned to the walls around us. "I live up on the sixth floor." I could see the confusion in his eyes. "Housing for a year is part of my benefits package. You didn't know?"

"Not a clue."

Now I was confused. "I figured it was standard practice."

"Actually, I've never heard of housing being offered to any employee."

I shrugged. "I guess there *are* some things that happen you don't know about." I nodded to the papers spread out in front of him. "So, what's first?"

"The theme," he said curtly.

"What's wrong with the theme? I thought we already discussed this." I sighed.

"The tagline is good, *Unmask Domestic Abuse.* We're calling it a masquerade ball. I want fancy script and elegance on the invitations. Make it clear this is a black-tie event, not a costume party."

He was like a dog with a bone about the whole costume party thing. Did he really think I was going to plan a Halloween party with a piñata and bobbing for apples? "You've been crystal clear on that point. When is this shindig anyway?" I used the casual term to ruffle his feathers.

"This *shindig* is in six weeks. We don't have time to fuck around," he scolded.

My eyes bulged. "Six weeks? That's cutting it really close." No wonder he was so uptight.

"Tell me something I don't know. Suzette was supposed to plan it, but she totally dropped the ball. No pun intended. That's why we need to work together to get it done."

I wanted to point out that he'd already wasted time by being an asshole but doing so was moot. I made a note in my portfolio. "I'll have Penny pull some invitation samples and we'll get it done by the end of the week." My pen tapped as I thought. "Was Brett serious about five thousand a ticket?"

"Yeah. The big rollers have no problem dropping that kind of cash. They write it off anyway," he said without looking up.

Unbelievable. I couldn't even imagine what that kind of wealth was like. Penny and I were definitely not attending the event. If anything, we'd be behind the scenes making sure everything ran according to Trent's expectations. "How many does the ballroom accommodate?"

"Five hundred."

I did some quick calculations. "That's a long way from five million."

He stopped spinning his pen and pointed it at me. "That's why you'll have to give a great presentation. If you pull on their hearts, the purse strings will open."

"Me? Why would I do it? I'm a nobody. I can't even afford to attend the event."

"*Buzzz.* Wrong answer. You're Gianna Romano, event coordinator extraordinaire."

I frowned. "Are you making fun of me?"

"Not at all. If you want to be somebody, then you need to convince them you are. Ever heard the phrase *fake it 'til you make it?*"

I nodded.

"Being successful has as much to do with your mindset as your actions. It's not enough to want it, you need to believe it. You walk the walk and talk the talk."

I was stunned. Speechless. No one had ever believed in me. My family. My friends. Even my ex-husband. They all thought I was overly ambitious. All my life I'd waited for someone to encourage me, and the person who finally did barely knew me. I didn't know what to say.

The door burst open, and Tom stumbled inside carrying two white take-out bags. "Sorry it took me so long, Mr. Dorsey. They were super crowded, and your food wasn't ready. I should have called it in sooner."

Trent grabbed the bags. "It's fine, Tom. Thank you. If you'd get a Diet Coke for Miss Romano, that would be great."

"I'm on it." He disappeared as fast as he'd arrived.

"You know what I drink?"

"I know more than your bra size, Gia," Trent said with a smirk.

I rolled my eyes. Just when I thought he was taking me seriously, he had to go and ruin it. Reaching for one of the bags, I pulled out my Pad Thai and unwrapped a set of chopsticks. My stomach rumbled as the spicy aroma spread throughout the room. I cinched a shrimp between the sticks and shoved it in my mouth. My eyes closed as I moaned, savoring the flavors bursting on my tongue. "Mmmm. So good. Total foodgasm." It'd been a while since I'd eaten Thai, absolutely too long.

A throat clearing pulled me out of the spicy-shrimp haze. Tom held out a twenty-ounce bottle. "Here's your Coke, Ms. Romano."

"Thank you." He continued watching me as I swallowed from the bottle.

"That's all, Tom," Trent snapped. "Why don't you take off for the day?"

"But it's only four thirty. I'm still working on that report you wanted."

"You can finish tomorrow. Shut the door on your way out."

"Yes, sir." The door closed with a soft click.

Trent dug into the other bag, pulling out his food. "Seriously? Are you trying to make the kid come in his pants?"

I held a hand over my lips as I swallowed. "Sorry. It's so good."

"Let's focus on the event." He twisted noodles around his chopsticks and shoved them in his mouth.

84

We worked for the next few hours, going over details, making notes, and creating a to-do list. I had no idea how we'd get everything accomplished in a matter of weeks. I was good, but not that good.

"I need a break." I pushed away from the table and stretched my back. Sitting in one place for too long wasn't my thing. I was a mover.

"Do you want to stop for the night?" Trent asked while loosening his tie and pulling it off. He folded it neatly on the table and undid the top button of his shirt. It was a normal man thing to do, but it sparked a fire in my belly.

I turned away from him and paced in front of the window, begging the sensation to go away. I kicked off my heels and wiggled my toes, working out the kinks. My feet were swollen and there was no way they'd fit back into my shoes. Trent raised an eyebrow as he watched me. I looked down at my painted toes and grimaced. "I should have asked if you cared if I took my shoes off."

"It's fine. I've seen your feet before, Gia."

Yes, of course he had. He'd seen a whole lot more than my feet. There was that spark again. "Still, it was rude. We're working."

He chuckled. "Technically, we've been off the clock for almost two hours. We can quit if you want to."

I shook my head. "I'm not a quitter. I'm here because I'm not afraid of hard work. You don't need to coddle me."

"If you were a quitter, you would have walked out the first day when you realized who I was. I'm not coddling you." Trent unbuttoned his cuffs and rolled his shirtsleeves up his forearms. A bit of ink peeked out from beneath the fabric. I'd noticed it the night we spent together but was too busy being completely satisfied by two men to discern what it was. I stared at him as heat crept up my neck at the memory. He cocked his head to the side. "What?"

I padded across the carpet in my bare feet, sat in the chair, and tucked one foot under my butt. "About that…"

"About what?"

I waved a hand in the air. "You know." He looked at me blankly, making me explain myself. "What happened…" I motioned between us. "I don't do stuff like that. It was my first night in Vegas… and… I shouldn't have."

Trent chuckled. "You're allowed to do what you want. There's no judgment on my part. I'm not sorry it happened. Are you?"

Was I? Now that was the question. It was the best sex of my life. I awoke sore and completely satisfied. Being with John so long, I'd forgotten what great sex was. By the end of our marriage, we were more roommates than husband and wife.

If I was being honest, waking to an empty bed was what bothered me the most. I mean, I knew what a one-night stand was, but I'd never had one before. I don't know what I was expecting but finding myself alone at the end was disappointing.

"I told you I didn't regret it. I just don't like how awkward everything is."

Trent inched his hand toward mine, the tip of his finger skimming the side of it. "That's my fault. I didn't know how to act when you showed up in the conference room. Throwing it in your face was wrong."

My skin prickled from his touch. "Can we…"

"Am I interrupting?"

Trent slid his hand away as I jumped. My heart beat like a teenager that'd been caught making out in the back seat of a car. It was ridiculous. Nothing happened. Nothing was going to happen. Trent was my boss. I'd be smart to remember that.

He leaned back casually and stared at his brother. "You're not interrupting at all. Miss Romano and I were going over plans for the fundraiser."

So, I was back to being Miss Romano? Of course, I was. He's your boss, I reminded myself again.

He's your boss.

He's your boss.

He's. Your. BOSS! Pull it together and be professional.

"Is that so?" Hunter asked, lifting a brow.

I took in the room from his perspective. The empty take-out containers strewn across the table. Trent's tie removed and shirt unbuttoned. My shoes left carelessly on the floor. My cheeks, I was sure were tinted red. It looked bad.

"Is there something you wanted?"

Hunter eased into the room despite Trent's cool demeanor. "Just checking on my brother. Didn't expect you to have company."

"Miss Romano isn't company. We're working." Trent held up my proposal with all its scribbled notes and *X*'s in bright red. I'd been so proud when I turned it in, but now it looked as pathetic as a fifth grader's book report.

Hunter turned and smiled at me. "Of course, she's a member of Mystique now. How are you liking Vegas?"

Why did I feel like this was a trick question? Surely, Trent didn't tell him about our tryst. I pasted on a smile. "It's been fine. I haven't done much exploring yet, but I'll get to it."

"And the job?"

"It's perfect. Everything I could have hoped for." So, that wasn't exactly the truth, but it seemed like the right thing to say under the circumstances.

"Good. Let's hope it stays that way. I trust my brother is treating you well?"

Something was off. Very off. "Extremely professional."

Trent tossed the pen he was spinning onto the table. "Are you finished with the inquisition? Miss Romano and I have a lot of work to finish."

Hunter picked up a cardboard container from the table and tossed it in the trash. "I wouldn't want to interrupt your *work*," he quipped. "And, Gia? I'd love to show you Vegas and all it has to offer. I think you'll find the amenities are quite pleasurable." He straightened his tie and gave me a piercing gaze. "I'd enjoy watching you try to take it all in."

I blinked. *Did he proposition me?* Chills ran down my spine. Both these men thought I was there solely for their amusement. I was a fool to think someone would actually take me seriously. "Do you mind if we call it quits for the night? I think I'm on overload." I closed my laptop and gathered my papers without waiting for a reply.

Trent's lips pressed into a firm line. "I seem to have lost my motivation as well. I'll see you tomorrow."

"Tomorrow," I agreed. "Nice seeing you again, Hunter." Brushing past him, I scurried down the hall and out the glass doors toward the elevator. I pushed the button frantically, begging for the car to arrive. When the doors opened, I stepped in on my bare feet and leaned against the wall.

What the hell was that?

Chapter 14
Trent

"Are you insane?"

Hunter smirked at me. "I have no idea what you're talking about."

I stood and stepped into his personal space. Enough of his bullshit. "You're kidding me, right? That was totally inappropriate."

He laughed. "Oh, that's rich. You're giving me a lecture on inappropriate while sitting here sharing egg foo yong."

"First of all, it was Thai food. Secondly, it was a working dinner. Thirdly, it's none of your fucking business."

"That's where you're wrong." He cocked his head at me. "It is my business. I've made it my personal responsibility to make sure you keep your dick out of that smart mouth of hers. I'm sure I could take care of her splendidly. Which, I might add, I have absolutely no problem with, unless you'd like to hand over your office keys now and save me the trouble."

I took another step forward. "Not going to happen, brother dearest. This has been my destiny since the day I was born. You showing up unexpectedly doesn't change that. My mother may have taken you in, but you'll always be a bastard."

"Careful. You're starting to sound threatened. I can't help it if your mother couldn't keep her husband satisfied."

My fingers curled into a fist and plowed into his face. My vision blurred in a haze of red as I hit him again. And a third time, just for good measure, that knocked him to the floor.

Hunter wiped the blood from his nose and laughed, his cheek already puffy and red. "There he is… the guy with no self-control. How long 'til you lose your control with Gia? I bet it's killing you. I'm happy to take her off your hands." He pushed to standing and touched his bruised face. "By the way, you hit like a pussy. I'll be watching," he said with a wink before leaving.

I slammed the door behind him. *Son of a bitch!* It'd been a long time since I'd punched him, but this time it was totally justified. My mom was off-limits. The woman was a saint for putting up with all she had over the years. He should have been grateful. Instead, he was a disrespectful little prick.

I shook out my arms and rubbed at the tender skin on my knuckles. Hunter was a problem. A huge problem. What was he doing creeping around the office at this time of night? He was usually the first to leave, God forbid he put in any extra time or actually try to earn his place in the family business. I paced in front of the window as I thought about my predicament.

There was no easy option. A riddle with no answer.

Pursue Gia and lose my job or keep my job and lose the woman. A woman who went running because the Dorsey brothers skeeved her out. It would take a while to convince her I was interested in more than sex.

Stop! Rewind!

I was interested in more than sex? When had that happened? Maybe it was the bold confidence she exuded despite the way we met. Maybe it was the way she had no problem putting me in my place. Or maybe it was the way she attended to details and fought for what she wanted. The desire she had to elevate herself through hard work.

I admired all those things.

Admiration was not the basis for a relationship. And why was I thinking about a relationship? I didn't do relationships. I didn't do dates in the traditional sense.

I fucked. Down and dirty with no strings and no complications.

So, why couldn't I get the redheaded complication out of my mind? There was something about her that pulled at me no matter how hard I tried to push it away.

Her black heels sat abandoned in the middle of my office. I scooped them from the floor and dialed the hotel front desk. Armed with her room number and the excuse of returning her shoes, I headed to the elevator. I should have dropped her shoes in her office and been done with it, but the way she left in a flurry after Hunter's proposition left me unsettled.

When the elevator dinged on the sixth floor, I headed to the right, where the efficiency suites were located. Standing outside her room, my heart thudded. It was ridiculous. I was returning her shoes. Nothing else.

With a quick rap on her door, I waited. And waited. And waited. Like a creeper, I pressed my ear against the door and listened to the soft sound of her television. Taking a deep breath, I knocked again.

The door cracked open, and Gia peeked through the narrow opening. "Trent?"

"Hi."

She bit her bottom lip. "I'm sorry I ran out so quickly. The long day…"

"I'm not worried about that." There was no way I would let her apologize for her reaction to Hunter's crude behavior. I held up her shoes. "You left these."

"Oh." The door closed momentarily while she undid the safety latch. When it opened fully, she reached for the shoes. "Thank you. You didn't have to do that." She looked adorable in shorts and an oversized T-shirt with her hair piled on top of her head in a messy knot. She seemed younger and more innocent. I found this version of her intriguing. It was like pulling the curtain back and seeing the real Gianna.

I smiled at her. "It's not a big deal. Luckily, you live close."

"True, but still…" She stuck her head out into the hallway and looked both ways. "How did you know which room was mine?"

91

"I've got my sources."

Her mouth quirked up on one side. "Of course you do. Did you want to come in?"

I hadn't planned on staying. It was supposed to be a quick drop-off, but the allure was too much to resist. "Only for a minute." I stepped inside and took in the small suite. It was artfully decorated with the Mystique flair but tiny as hell. The entire kitchen and sitting area would fit into my bedroom. Boxes were neatly stacked in the corners. A love seat and chair faced the television. Her laptop sat on the small table next to a bottle of wine and a nearly empty glass. "You're going to live here for a year? You're going to get claustrophobia."

Gia shuffled on her bare feet and clicked the television off. "It'll be fine. I don't need much." "Do you want something to drink? I have water, Diet Coke, or wine." She lifted her glass from the table and swallowed down the bit of liquid left in the bottom.

"Water would be great."

She took the few steps to the kitchen and returned with a bottle of Aquafina. "Why are you really here, Trent? You could have left my shoes in my office."

I took a sip of my water and sat on the love seat with a sigh. "I could have, but I wanted to check on you."

She sat on the chair across from me, tucking her legs underneath her butt. "Check on me why?"

I reached up and grabbed the back of my neck, digging my fingers into the tight muscles. "Because... Hunter..."

"Treated me like a whore?" she finished, reaching for the bottle on the table and refilling her glass.

I cringed. "Yes. An apology was needed."

She eyed me over the rim of her glass. "Did you tell him about us?"

"I would never. What happened is none of his business or anyone else's."

"Actually, it is one other person's business." Her eyebrow quirked up.

"Brett would never say a word, especially to Hunter. The guy is a vault. You have no worries with him."

"Well, that makes me feel a tad bit better." She tapped her nails on the glass and sighed. "So, either your brother's a douchebag or I give off the wrong vibes."

I sat forward and rested my arms on my legs. "Half brother. And he's been an entitled prick since the day he came into my life. You didn't do anything wrong."

Gia threw her head back and laughed. "Everything I've done since I got here has been wrong. Starting with sleeping with the one man I shouldn't have... my boss."

My lips quirked up. "It was an unforeseen complication, but it wasn't a mistake."

She harrumphed. "It isn't your career on the line."

"Actually, it is," I admitted.

"You're the boss. Explain."

"The boss's son. And I don't have a stellar reputation. My future at Mystique depends on me not sleeping with the female employees."

"Too late." She giggled.

I ran a hand through my hair. "No kidding. It would have been easier if you quit." The words spilled out with more bluntness than I intended.

Gia straightened her spine. "I'm not quitting."

I shook my head. "I don't expect you to. And I don't want you to. Truth be told, I like having you around."

"Is that so?"

"Yes."

"And why is that?"

"Are you fishing for compliments, Miss Romano?"

She shrugged. "What can I say? I'm a compliments kind of girl."

"Fine." I ticked the reasons on my fingers. "You're bold. You're smart. You're not too hard on the eyes. And I wouldn't mind getting to know you better."

Gia's lips pressed into a firm line. "You're arrogant, bossy, and a control freak. But"—she held up a finger—"I think underneath all that, there might be a good guy hiding and I wouldn't mind getting to know him better too."

I slapped my hands on my legs and stood. "Perfect. It's a plan."

93

She frowned. "What's a plan?"

I motioned between the two of us. "Getting to know each other better. Friday night I'm going to give you the Vegas tour." I wagged a finger at her. "Purely platonic, so don't be getting any ideas." Although I had plenty of ideas running around in my head. Most of which consisted of her naked underneath me.

Gia stood and placed her wineglass on the table. "It sounds more like an order than an invitation."

"It's a date." I waved my hand back and forth. "Kind of."

"So, *kind of* a date? What about work? If someone sees us together…" She worried her lip between her teeth.

"It's a big city. Besides, it's puuurely platonic," I said with a wink. "But, just in case, how about we keep it on the down-low?"

"So, I'm going to be *your* dirty little secret," she said with her hands planted on her voluptuous hips.

"Think of it as a private meeting. Two friends getting to know each other." There I went, throwing *friends* into the universe again. If I was lucky, it'd turn into a *friends-with-benefits* situation.

"It's a terrible idea," she said.

"The worst." We stood awkwardly mulling over the implications of the deal we'd made. The silence stretched between us like a palpable force pushing us apart yet pulling us together. "I'll see you tomorrow," I finally said, walking toward the door. If I didn't leave now, I'd be tempted to do something stupid. "And don't worry about Hunter. I've taken care of it."

"Thanks for bringing up my shoes. See you tomorrow." The door clicked closed behind me.

This could quite possibly be the most foolish thing I'd ever done. Or the smartest. It was yet to be determined.

Chapter 15
Gia

A private meeting, my ass!

Why I agreed, I didn't know. It was a horrible, awful, ridiculous idea. Self-sabotage at its finest. An affair with my boss was strictly against company guidelines. I could lose my job, my dignity, and my reputation. I doubted the Onyx in Chicago would take me back if I got canned in Vegas.

Today was Tuesday, plenty of time to renege on our deal. I'd simply tell Trent I changed my mind. That it wasn't worth the risk.

Telling him *no* was the right thing to do.

Then why did my stomach sink at the thought of it?

Deep down, I was more attracted to Trent than I wanted to admit. It was his charm and charisma that got me into trouble in the first place. And let's not forget his sexy little smirk and the memory of his five-o'clock shadow rubbing against the insides of my thighs.

I sighed, thinking about the things I was giving up.

That's why it's called a one-night stand, Gia.

One and done.

Rearview mirror.

Put it in the past.

Woman up and do what needs to be done.

But all I could think about was the sexual tension between us last night. I looked down at my feet and the shoes that brought him to my room. I should have never left them behind. Then Trent wouldn't have shown up at my door.

"Mr. Dorsey would like to see you in his office."

I was lost in my own thoughts. "Excuse me?"

Tom pushed his glasses up his nose. "Mr. Dorsey said you didn't finish your meeting last night and I was to come and fetch you."

Fetch me? He seriously couldn't have used those words. I wasn't a dog. "I see." I gathered my laptop and notes only to find Tom still there. "Is there a reason you're standing in my doorway?"

"Mr. Dorsey said I was to escort you to his office. I'm just following orders, ma'am."

Tom's manners were impeccable, but it seemed I wasn't the only one being treated like a dog. The kid needed to grow a set of balls. "Fine." I followed him down the hall, my heels clicking on the marble. "Tom, would you be a dear and *fetch* me a cup of coffee? Two sugars, one cream."

He held Trent's office door open for me like a gentleman. "Sure thing, Ms. Romano. Mr. Dorsey, would you like coffee as well?"

I glared at the man behind the desk. "Yes, Trent, would you like Tom to *fetch* you some coffee?"

"That would be great," he said without looking up from his computer and totally oblivious to my irritation.

My toe tapped impatiently as Tom scurried away like a trained puppy. This all seemed like a game to my boss. The man was used to getting what he wanted and what he wanted right now was me. The fact that I was forbidden only made the challenge more appealing.

Well, I had news for him... he wasn't going to get what he wanted this time. I set my papers and laptop on the table, taking up as much room as possible. A clear barrier between the two of us. I checked my email while I waited for Trent, as he seemed too busy to even notice I existed when last night he was all up in my personal space. I didn't have the time or patience for his games.

Tom returned with our coffee and disappeared quickly. I was half-finished with mine before Trent gave me the time of day. "Are you ready to get started?"

I gave him a steely stare. "I've been ready for the last fifteen minutes. I have other things I could be doing. My time is as valuable as yours." I pointed to my wrist. "Ticktock, mister."

He pulled his chair next to mine, pushing my papers to the side. "And what is it that needs your attention so badly besides being here with me?"

I saw what he was doing. Trying to get me flustered with his subtle innuendo. "I'm writing a request for items for our silent auction. I'll be sending it out to major players in Nevada and the surrounding states. There's a lot of money along the coast. We just need to capture some of it."

"I agree. Can I see what you've written?"

I didn't appreciate being micromanaged, but he was my boss, so I swiveled my laptop in his direction. "It's a rough draft," I said, afraid it would get marked up like my proposal.

"I know." It seemed to take him forever, as he leaned closer, to read the three short paragraphs. A quirk of his lip, a twitch of his nose, and two *hmms* later he said, "It's good. A minor tweak and it'll be perfect."

It was high praise from a man who was hard to please. "What kind of tweak?" I wasn't so egotistical to think I didn't have room for improvement. Vegas was a whole different ballgame than I was used to.

His hands hovered over the keyboard. "May I?"

"Of course." I watched as he deleted and inserted new text into the signature of the document, shaking my head at what he typed. "That's not correct."

"It was selling you short. It's better now." He gave me a wolfish smile.

I swiveled the computer back and started to erase what he'd written. "It's not true and I won't be accused of false representation."

Trent gently grabbed my hands. Tingles crept up my arms and my heart pattered faster. It was dangerous being this close to him. "Leave it. Let me worry about the details."

Worrying was what I did best. "I'll throw you under the bus in a heartbeat. I won't take the fall for this."

"I'm sure you will, but I'm the COO and it's my call." He chuckled as he picked up the paperwork from yesterday. "Let's finish going over your proposal. I have more ideas to add."

"Director of events and entertainment?" Penny let out a low whistle. "Somebody's moving up in the world."

I swiped the document from her hand. "It's a matter of semantics. Same position, same pay."

"With a much classier title. If I didn't know better, I'd say Trent has a little crush on you." She tapped a finger on her chin. "It totally makes sense now, the way he gave you such a hard time last week. It's no different than a boy pulling a girl's pigtails on the playground. Men never really grow up."

This train of thought needed to be caboshed before it ran off the tracks. "Don't be ridiculous. The new title looks better for the company, plain and simple. It makes the request seem more official than *event coordinator*." I grabbed my purse from the desk drawer. "Are you ready for lunch?"

Penny shuffled nervously. "I actually have a lunch date."

I dropped my purse and sat on the edge of my desk. "I didn't know you were seeing someone. Have you been holding out on me?"

She waved her hand at me. "It's nothing serious. As a matter of fact, I'm probably making more out of it than it really is." She tugged on the bottom of her blouse, smoothing out the wrinkles. "Do I look all right?"

"Penny, you're cute as a button. Any man would be lucky to spend time with you."

She slumped. "Ugh! I don't want to be cute. I want to be sexy and sophisticated like you."

"You're perfect the way you are. Don't think you have to change for a man."

Penny sighed. "It's not just any man. It's Brett. We're meeting so we can go over the big players for the guest list. Am I crazy to hope he could see me as something more?"

That was surprising news. I never pictured Penny with Brett, but it was totally possible. Penny was smart, sweet, pretty, and driven. She simply lacked confidence. There wasn't a single reason he shouldn't like her, but men like him were accustomed to something more refined. "You're not crazy. May I?" I motioned to her outfit.

"Please. Whatever you think will help."

"To be clear, you don't need any improvements, but I think you can capitalize more on your assets." I took her glasses off the top of her head and fluffed up her dark curls. "Take your jacket off and have a seat."

Penny quickly pulled it off and sat pristinely in the padded chair.

I opened my purse and pulled out my touch-up kit. "You have beautiful eyes. I want to make them pop." I lined her eyes in dark strokes, defining them and making the green stand out. Adding a couple coats of mascara, her naturally long lashes framed her eyes in sensuous fans. A touch of blush and a pale-pink lip gloss completed the look. I stood back and admired my work. Something was still missing. "Stand up for me."

Penny stood and did a dainty twirl.

I undid the top two buttons on her blouse, revealing the teensiest bit of cleavage. "What size shoes do you wear?"

She crinkled her nose. "An eight."

"Perfect." I slipped the heels off my feet and nudged them in front of her with my toe. "Try these on."

The shoes made her three inches taller. "I don't wear heels." Penny tested them out by taking a few laps around the room. "They're kinda comfortable."

I opened the door to the coat closet and motioned for Penny to take a look in the mirror attached to the inside. "What do you think?"

"I look stylish and chic," she said, smiling. "Thank you. I hope Brett likes it."

"What Brett thinks isn't important. He doesn't get to decide if you feel good about yourself or not. Confidence comes from in here." I tapped on her chest. "You're beautiful. Own it."

"Have I told you what a great boss you are?"

I gave her a hug. "I hope I'm more than your boss. I'd like to think we're friends."

"Definitely friends."

As we stood embracing, all I could think was, *she can never know I slept with Brett.*

Chapter 16
Trent

Midafternoon, my mother stopped by the office dressed in a designer linen pantsuit. Even in her late fifties, she had an air of grace and beauty. Underneath it all, she was a shark with a keen mind for business. Her lack of involvement in the day-to-day operations of Mystique was by choice, not because she didn't have the skills.

I stood and gave her a hug. "To what do I owe the pleasure?" I asked, kissing her cheek.

"Do I need a reason to visit my son?" She held me by the arms and inspected me like she did when I was a kid. "I think you're getting more handsome."

"And I think you're biased. You say that every time." I laughed.

"I can't help it if it's true," she said with a shrug, sitting in one of the chairs opposite my desk.

I pulled up another, so we were face to face, to give her the respect she deserved. My mom was my biggest supporter, even when I made questionable decisions. And I'd made a shit ton of them. "Are you excited for your vacation?"

"It'll be more work than play, but yes. I can't wait to sit on the beach in Hawaii and drink a mai tai. I'll get your dad to take me to one of those dolphin preserves. Did I ever tell you we swam with dolphins on our honeymoon?" she asked with a dreamy look in her eyes.

My parents' marriage was strained since Hunter showed up, but I wanted to believe they still loved each other. "I didn't know that."

"We used to have the best time together. I met him when I was fifteen and he was seventeen. Our parents pushed us together, but in the end, it was our choice. I want to get back some of that spark."

"Hawaii's a good place for that."

"Hawaii, New Orleans, Biloxi, Miami, New York, Chicago... we're making the rounds. It's going to be exhausting."

"I'm sure you'll have some fun too."

"I'll make my own fun. Now, enough about me. What about you? You work too hard. Are you seeing anyone?"

I could barely keep a straight face. "I date plenty of women, Mom."

She pressed her lips together. "Hmmm. I'm not sure our definition of dating is the same, Trent. I'm not talking about *hooking up*," she finger quoted. "I'm talking about a real date where you pick a woman up at her home and take her somewhere. Possibly buy her dinner. Get to know her."

I cringed at the words *hooking up*. She meant fucking and the last thing I wanted to talk to my mother about was sex. "I have someone I'm interested in, but no date yet. There are a million reasons we shouldn't go out." Like being her boss. Like losing my legacy. Like giving Hunter another reason to stab me in the back.

"It sounds like excuses. I'd like to have grandchildren one day. You need to get serious with your love life."

I pulled at the collar of my shirt, which felt like a choker around my neck. "There's no hurry."

"Maybe not for you, but there is for me. I'd like to see you settle down with a nice woman before I die."

"You're not anywhere close to dying, Mom. Stop being so dramatic." I rolled my eyes.

"I'm not being dramatic. You never know what's going to happen. One minute you're here." She snapped her fingers. "The next minute you're gone. I could get eaten by a shark in Hawaii."

Now she really was being dramatic. "That's very doubtful."

Two sharp knocks came at my door before it swung open. "Trent, I had a question about…" Gia looked up from the paper she was holding, her eyes wide. "I'm sorry. I didn't know you had a meeting."

I scanned her from head to curiously bare toes. I waved her in with a flick of my wrist. "It's fine. Come meet my mother."

If she seemed surprised before, she was horrified now. "I can come back. I didn't mean to interrupt."

"You're not interrupting. As a matter of fact, you might be saving me." My mother scowled.

Gia padded in on her bare feet, something that was becoming way too familiar.

Twitching her head to the side, my mother asked, "Where are your shoes, dear?" It was a good question. One I wondered the answer to also.

She wiggled her toes. "I loaned them to a friend. It was kind of an emergency. She'll be bringing them back after lunch."

I quirked an eyebrow at her, not sure if it was the truth or an elaborate story she concocted.

My mom smiled at Gia. "You're a good friend. Luckily, she didn't need your blouse."

"I'm not that good of a friend." Gia stuck her hand out. "I'm Gia, the new event coordinator. It's nice to meet you, Mrs. Dorsey."

"Director of entertainment and events," I corrected.

Gia blushed. "It's not official."

Holding Gia's outstretched hand in both of hers, my mother said, "It's Rose, and the pleasure is all mine. Come sit with us."

She looked unsure if she should accept the invitation, but I quickly pulled another chair over and tapped the seat. This should be interesting. My mother was ferocious, and a tough critic. I'd never introduced her to a woman I'd dated, not that Gia and I were dating but it was closer than I'd been in years. My list of girlfriends could be written on the back of a postage stamp.

Gia gingerly sat and tried to hide her bare feet under the chair, even though we'd both seen them already.

"How are you liking Mystique, Gia? Has my son been treating you well?"

"I'm enjoying it. Everyone's been really nice and helpful."

It was the perfect answer for anyone other than my mother. "But?"

Gia sighed. "But it's been challenging. Things happen a little faster here than they did in Chicago. I thought I'd have more time to adjust before being thrown into the fire. The fundraiser is no joke. I've never done anything of this magnitude before. Penny, my assistant, has been a godsend. That's why I didn't have a problem loaning her my shoes."

My mom patted Gia's hand. "It's always good to have a great assistant." Then her eyes narrowed and focused on me. "Surely, Trent has helped you get acclimated. I can't imagine he'd throw you into the fundraiser alone in the first week. That would be very ungentlemanly and certainly not how he was raised."

It was part question and part accusation. If ever Gia wanted to throw me under the bus, as she promised she would, now was her chance. Beads of perspiration rolled down the back of my neck.

With her eyes glued to mine, she said, "Oh, I felt like I knew him before I even started. To say he was welcoming wouldn't do him justice. His expectations were very clear. Very professional," she drawled.

I leaned back in my chair, "What can I say? My mother raised me right."

"I can't take all the credit," my mom said. "Trent's always been headstrong. When he sees something he wants, he goes after it."

"I'm beginning to learn that."

My mother clapped her hands together. "I'm very excited about the fundraiser. I can't wait to see what you two come up with. What's the theme?"

Gia straightened. "It's a masquerade ball with a New Orleans flair. We're going all out. Trent thought masks were childish, but I've convinced him it's going to be classy and elegant."

I straightened my tie and gave her a stern glare. "We don't have all the details worked out yet."

"Yes, Trent has suggested a lot of changes."

"Modifications. We're still sticking with your original vision."

"If my vision was blurry. Although, I'll admit you do have *some* brilliant ideas.

"That's why I'm the boss."

"Yes, and I'm the event coordinator."

"Director of entertainment and events."

"It's not official."

"It is if I say so. I always get what I want."

"Is that so?" Gia asked with a lift of her manicured brow.

"It is," I assured her. I wasn't even sure what we were talking about anymore. The title. The event. Or us. Because the more she argued with me, the more I wanted the latter to be true.

"Well, that sounds spectacular," my mother interrupted with another clap of her hands. "I'll be on pins and needles to see how this all works out."

Gia's head spun in her direction, as if she had just remembered my mom was in the room. With a smile pasted on, her professional face was back in place. "It was wonderful to meet you, but I must get back to work. So much to do," she said with a smile. "I hope I get to see you again."

"Oh, I'm counting on it," my mother answered.

The redheaded firecracker stood and smoothed her skirt down, then strolled to the door as if she were wearing three-inch heels. "Please let me know when you're available, Mr. Dorsey. I'd like to go over your *modifications.*"

"I'll have Tom come *fetch* you," I quipped back, not able to resist the dig.

She rolled her eyes and walked out the door.

My attention turned back to my mother who was sitting smugly with a Cheshire cat grin. "What?"

"She's lovely."

My jaw dropped. "Lovely? Did you not hear how she talked to me? She's a total pain in my ass."

My mother shrugged nonchalantly. "She's a strong, independent woman who challenges you. It's good for you. Pretty too. More than I could have asked for."

I wasn't sure what that meant, but I considered it her blessing. Pain in the ass or not, I wanted Miss Sassy Pants, a.k.a. Gianna Romano.

Chapter 17
Gia

"How did your lunch go?"

Penny hobbled into my office and kicked off my shoes. "I don't know how you wear these all day long. My feet feel like they went through a meat grinder."

I chuckled. "They take some getting used to. Try wedges, they have more support."

She fell into a chair and began rubbing her aching toes. "I'll stick with my flats."

"We'll work on it. Shoes aside, how was your lunch? You were gone for a while."

"Would it be crazy if I said I was in love with the man?" she asked with a dreamy look in her eyes.

"That was quick."

"I'm easy. What can I say?"

My eyebrows shot up to my hairline.

"Not that kind of easy, you perve," she said, picking up a pad of sticky notes from my desk and tossing them at me. "I mean I fall in love easily. It's a curse. I have the uncanny ability to fall in love with men who are completely out of my league."

"Who says he's out of your league?"

"You've seen him. He looks like a GQ model, and I look like this." She waved her hand up and down her body. "I'm living in a fantasy world."

"You're too hard on yourself," I insisted. "He could have come to the office and handed you a list of names instead of taking you to lunch. I think that shows promise."

"Well…" she said, reaching into her purse. "He did give me this." Penny held up a blue-and-green plastic ball.

"What is it?"

She shook the ball and a bell jingled inside. "It's for Fred, so he doesn't get upset when I'm gone."

I giggled. "That's totally sweet. See. He was thinking about your pussy."

Penny gasped. "I can't believe you just said that!"

"I call it the way it is."

She sat there stone-faced, then burst out laughing. "Oh, my god! You're so bad." Her laughter was contagious and soon both of us were in hysterics.

A sharp knock on the partially opened door pulled my attention. "Am I interrupting?"

My hand flew up in front of my mouth. "What happened to your face?" The entire left side of Hunter's face was bruised purple and black. His eye and nose were swollen. His lip split, red and angry.

He gently touched the skin around his nose. "It looks worse than it feels. You should see the other guy."

I'd already seen the other guy. Trent's words echoed in my head. *Don't worry about Hunter. I've taken care of it.* The realization felt like liquid heat filling my chest and flowing to my extremities. No one had ever defended my honor before.

I cleared my throat. "Well, I'm glad you're okay." It was a lie. He deserved everything Trent rained down on him. "Is there something you need?"

"Two things actually." Hunter gave Penny a long, hard stare. "Do you mind?"

"Oh, right!" Penny gathered her purse, slipped her flats on, and scurried out the door.

"Was that really necessary?" I asked, annoyed he thought he had the authority to boss around my assistant. He probably did, but that was beside the point.

"I wanted to speak with you alone." He stepped inside my office and shut the door behind him. "First, I wanted to know if you needed any help with financials for the fundraiser. I can be a very valuable resource." He sauntered forward and sat on the edge of my desk like he owned the place. "Teach you all the ins and outs."

Ooooh gross! His pickup lines needed serious help. Obviously, Trent hadn't punched him hard enough. I faked a smile. "That's nice of you, but Trent already has everything in the works. You could ask him if he'd like help." I wanted as far out of the equation as possible.

"I'll do that." Hunter picked up a pen from my desk and started to twirl it like I'd seen Trent do on more than one occasion. His eyes bore into me like he could see beneath my clothes.

I tugged at the top of my blouse, closing the open gap. The way he stared at me made my skin prickle, and not in a good way. "Was there something else?"

"Huh?"

I stood from behind my desk, not comfortable with his height advantage. "You said there were two things."

"Right." He set the pen down. "I thought we could get a drink after work. Make up for the breakfast we missed."

The guy was killing me. "That's a nice offer, but I've got a ton of work to catch up on." I lifted the stack from the corner of my desk and let it drop with a thud. "Besides, I don't mix business with pleasure. It's probably not a good idea."

His jaw clenched. "It's only a drink, Gia."

This level of persistence unnerved me. Why couldn't he take no for an answer? "I realize that, but we wouldn't want people talking, would we? Especially after the Suzette scandal." Every reason I gave him, I should have been giving Trent. Hunter wasn't the real problem. I felt no urge to break company rules with him. No urge to jeopardize my career because of him. No urge to go down a rabbit hole I might not come out of.

"I'm not my brother," he snapped as he zoned in on my boobs.

I crossed my arms to give myself another layer of protection against his roving eyes. "I'm well aware of that."

It was a standoff, neither of us budging.

"What's going on here?" Trent's voice cut through the tension like a sharp knife.

I was so focused on his brother I hadn't even heard the door open. My shoulders sagged in relief. His timing couldn't have been more perfect. "I was just telling Hunter we have all the financials for the fundraiser covered."

"Is that right?" Trent questioned his brother.

Hunter smiled, the movement splitting his lip open. He wiped the drop of blood with his finger and licked it off. "That's right. I thought you might need a little intervention."

Trent stuffed his hands in his pockets. "Like Miss Romano said, it's all under control. I'll let you know if I need an *intervention*. I think sometimes you forget I have more seniority and experience than you."

Hunter chuckled an unamused laugh. "And I think you forget what's on the line. I'm already picking out new furniture."

"Don't fucking hold your breath." The two glared daggers at each other as I watched silently. There was a fuckton of animosity between the two. "Nice face, by the way," Trent said calmly.

"It was a cheap shot. It won't happen again." Hunter pushed off the desk and knocked Trent's shoulder with his on the way to the door. Then he stopped and shot his finger at me. "Let me know if you change your mind about that drink. All work and no play makes Gia a dull girl." The fucker had the audacity to wink at me on his way out.

I stomped past Trent in my bare feet and slammed the door shut. "At first, I felt bad when I saw his face, but you should have hit him harder. The guy doesn't know how to take no for an answer."

"Easy, killer. I'll handle him."

My hands flew in the air. "What are you going to do? Punch him in the face again? I'm sure your father would be thrilled. It's going to get me fired."

He took my hands and held them in his, gently running his thumbs across my knuckles. Lowering down, he looked into my eyes. "You're not getting fired."

That made me feel a little better, but then I remembered something else Hunter had said. "What did he mean about picking out new furniture? Are you getting fired?"

"No one's getting fired, Gia."

I wanted to believe him, but this whole situation had me wound up. "I don't think we should be seen together. No tour of Vegas. No *kind of* dates. No working in your office alone. No nothing."

"You're overreacting. I told you I'd handle it. We haven't done anything wrong."

"Yet."

Trent smirked at me. "Are you saying you'd like to do something wrong? That could be arranged."

I pulled my hands away from his and went back to my desk. Slipping back into my shoes, I put my professional face back on. "I don't want to do anything that might jeopardize my place here. Sleeping with you would do that."

He pushed his hands back in his pockets. "I don't recall saying anything about sleeping together. I offered to show you Vegas. I distinctly remember saying it was purely platonic."

My lips pursed. Maybe I read the signs wrong. There was no denying the chemistry between us, but Trent didn't want to lose his job any more than I did.

"It's two people exploring the city together. Nothing else," he repeated.

I mulled over his words. I really did want to get out and explore all the sights I could see from my hotel room window. Vegas was like nothing I'd ever seen before, and I'd only experienced a teeny part of it. Who better to show me around than someone who'd lived here his whole life? I sighed. "I'd like that. But..." I stepped to my computer and pulled up my schedule for the week. With the fundraiser, I hadn't been giving the other aspects of my job enough attention. "There's a show on Friday night and one on Saturday too. I need to be there to make sure everything runs smoothly." I looked at the name of the band. "I've never heard of them before. Social Proof?" I clicked around some more. "They're out of Seattle."

Trent came around the side of my desk and peered over my shoulder. "They've been here before. You don't have to be there."

"Huh?" I was totally distracted by the scent of his cologne. It took me back to the night we met in the bar. A night I hadn't been able to push from my mind, even if I knew I should.

He ran a hand over his face and through his closely-cropped beard. "My mother was right. I threw you right into the fire without proper training. Have a seat." He picked up my phone and barked at Tom, "Bring me the staffing for the event team. I'm in Miss Romano's office."

I sat in my plush chair, not because Trent told me to, but because suddenly I felt overwhelmed. "I don't understand. At the Onyx I was in charge of everything. Every detail depended on me."

"This isn't the Onyx."

Tom gave a quick knock and hurried in with a single sheet of paper. "Here you go, Mr. Dorsey."

Trent took it from him. "Thank you, Tom." He laid the paper on my desk. "This is the event team."

I hunched over my desk and inspected a list of twenty names and positions. "All these people work for you?" I couldn't believe Penny hadn't mentioned this before. Seemed like a detail I should have known about.

"Technically, they work for you. Everyone that performs here comes with their own crew, but these are our people that pull it all together. From lighting and sound specialists to security. Before every event they're already

112

prepped with all the details. There's nothing for you to do but schedule the entertainment and get the contracts signed. Penny handles the rest."

My hand ran over the list. "But I don't even know these people. Don't you think I should make an appearance?"

"It's unnecessary, but you can if it makes you feel better."

"It totally would."

"Then I'll come to the show with you."

"You don't have to do that," I insisted. I didn't want him to think I couldn't handle the pressure.

"I should. As a matter of fact, I should have better acquainted you with the job instead of riding you so hard."

My head snapped up.

He held a hand out in front of him. "That's not what I meant."

"Uh-huh. Sure you didn't."

Seemed like he couldn't get our night together out of his head either.

Chapter 18
Trent

"You're fucking unbelievable!"

I smiled at Hunter as he stormed into my office. "I don't have a clue what you're talking about."

"That's bullshit and you know it." He slammed a pile of papers on top of my desk.

"What's that?" I asked with a smirk.

"The performance report for the hotel in Albuquerque. Apparently, they need help with the books, so I'm being sent there for the next month." He scowled. "Kind of convenient, don't you think? With Dad leaving tomorrow, you'll be totally unsupervised."

Yes, I planted the seed in my father's head about sending Hunter away, and it was completely justified with the way he'd been harassing Gia. I stood and leaned forward on my desk. His arrogance and condescending tone, paired with the way he treated Gia, pushed me over the edge. "Listen, you entitled little fuck, you need to start minding your own goddamn business. Wherever Dad decides to put you, is your issue. You want to think you're better than everyone else around here? Then start proving your worth and quit whining like a prissy little bitch every time something doesn't go your way. You've disrespected Gia one too many fucking times. When you come back, you better do it with a new fucking attitude because I've taken more crap from you than I should have. FYI… I'm the heir to this company, built by both sets of MY grandparents. I don't need, nor want, your supervision. My name was already on the door before you were born. Unless you want to be working in Albuquerque permanently, I'd suggest you heed my warning."

"Are you threatening me?" he asked with a sneer.

"No more than you've threatened me. The difference is I have the power to make it happen. Now, if I were you, I'd go pack my bags. Ticktock or you'll miss your flight." I had Tom book him on the seven o'clock tonight. The sooner he was gone the better. A temporary fix was better than no fix at all.

Hunter slammed his fist on my desk. "This isn't over! You fuck up and I'll know about it. I promise you that."

He'd tap danced on my last nerve. "Get out! I'm not discussing this any further." I waved my fingers at him. "Buh-bye. Have a nice trip."

My brother left, but not before flipping me off. I rolled my shoulders and shook out my arms, irritated with myself for letting him wind me up like that. He brought out the worst in me. Always had.

Gia peeked her head in my office. "Are you alright?"

"I'm fine. Why wouldn't I be?" I snapped harsher than intended.

She stepped inside and gently shut the door behind her. "I heard you yelling all the way from my office. I'm pretty sure everyone else did too."

I ran a hand down my face. "Fuck."

"Are you sure you're okay?"

With Hunter gone, I could finally relax. "I am now. You won't have to worry about my jerkoff brother bothering you for a while."

"Oh?"

"I had my father send him to our hotel in New Mexico."

"Seriously? You had him exiled?"

"Temporarily. Unfortunately, he'll be back in a few weeks." Her lips turned down and she bit her lip. "I thought you'd be happier."

"I am happy. It's… I'm afraid this is going to make things worse. He's going to want revenge when he gets back."

"Has anybody ever told you that you worry too much?"

"I can't help it. There's a lot going on in here," she said, tapping her temple.

"Come here." I held my hand out to her. She walked tentatively toward me and took my outreached hand in hers. "I want to show you something." I walked her over to the tinted window overlooking the casino. "See all those people down there?"

Like before, she pressed her face to the window in awe.

"They came to Vegas to try their luck. Some of them will win and some of them will lose. They took a gamble, same as you. The difference is you're not depending on the spin of a wheel or a roll of the dice. You're making your own luck. You came here with a purpose, and you haven't let anything deter you from working toward your dream, not even me. If you can handle all the shit I've piled on you, then you sure as hell can handle Hunter. Don't let him ruin the experience."

"I have a confession," she said, looking more vulnerable than I'd ever seen her. "No one has ever believed in me. My family, my friends, even my ex-husband, they all thought I was reaching beyond my station in life. They couldn't understand why I wasn't happy. My grandpa worked in the factory. My dad works in the factory. My uncles all work in the factory. I watched them work their asses off for a paycheck that barely covered the bills. My mom works in a gift shop selling trinkets to tourists that think Waukegan is cute. I'm not putting them down. There's nothing wrong with that life, but I want more. I was the first one in my family to go to college and I promised myself I wouldn't waste it. I didn't want to be the woman who cooks and cleans with a baby on her hip. Living where a big night out is watching the ballgame at the corner bar while drinking a beer." She tugged on the ends of her red hair and motioned to the dress she was wearing. "This is who I wanted to be. So, when you said *fake it 'til you make it*, that's all I've been doing. Nobody expects me to succeed. They're waiting for me to come home with my tail between my legs. And deep down, I'm afraid they're going to be right."

116

I'd seen that simple girl the other night when I returned her shoes, and she intrigued me as much as the woman standing in front of me. I cupped her face in my palms and turned her bright-blue eyes toward mine. This woman, who was so fierce on the outside, was a nervous mess on the inside. "You can be whoever you want to be."

"Pfft. That's easy to say when you have money and a family who backs you. I've just got me."

"It's two sides of the same coin. Everyone expects me to take over this company one day. They expect me to be like my father and have all my shit together. But the reality is I've made mistakes and I'm probably going to make more. I will take over this business eventually, but it's going to be on my terms."

"I hadn't thought of it that way."

"And you don't just have yourself, you have me too." I leaned down and pressed my lips against hers. She was frozen at first, but eventually her lips moved with mine and it was a thousand times better than I remembered. Her arms wrapped around my neck, and she let out a little moan that had my dick standing at attention.

Gia reluctantly pulled away. "We shouldn't be doing this."

I captured her lips again. "We definitely shouldn't, but I can't resist you."

"We could lose our jobs," she whispered.

"I won't let that happen. Let me take you out Friday after the show. No expectations. Just us getting to know each other. Let's see where this takes us." There I was, proposing going slow when all I'd ever done was jump into bed with woman after woman.

"Okay, but I don't want it to make things weird between us."

I laughed. "Weirder than it already is? I doubt that's possible." I pecked her on the lips again. "We'll be totally professional."

"We're not having sex."

"Absolutely not."

Resisting her was going to be a challenge, but when she gave in it would be worth the wait.

117

Chapter 19
Gia

My lips still tingled from the kiss Trent and I shared on Wednesday. True to his word, he was totally professional the rest of the week. We completed the invitations and Trent was having them hand-delivered across the city. Penny sent out dozens of requests for the silent auction. The band was booked, the menu finalized, and the decorations ordered.

Penny crashed into my office, which now looked more like a war room with papers and sticky notes stuck all over one of the walls. It was old school, but I couldn't work with everything crammed into files on my computer. I needed to see it. Visualize it.

She fell into one of the chairs, a pen tucked into the mass of curls piled on top of her head. "I'm fucking exhausted."

I laughed at her dramatics. "Do you want to go back to getting me coffee and answering emails?"

"Hell no! I thrive off this shit."

I laughed again. "That's what I thought. Go home and get some rest, then be ready to hit it hard again on Monday."

Penny waggled her eyebrows at me. "I have a date."

"With Brett?" I gasped.

She nodded like a bobblehead. "He's picking me up at my apartment so he can meet Fred, then he's taking me to a fancy French restaurant. I've never had French food before except for french fries and French toast; however, I doubt that will be on the menu."

"Good guess. Order something with chicken. Chicken is always safe." I wished I could have been as open as Penny was about going on a date with Brett, but no one could know Trent and I were involved, whatever that meant. The kiss we shared in his office wasn't what I expected after I poured my heart out to him. I expected him to think I was weak and incapable, but he surprised me by being encouraging and empathetic. I shouldn't have been shocked. I'd seen glimpses of his soft side, but usually his tyrannical behavior overshadowed it. Now, I wondered if it was all an act. If he was being what people expected of him.

Penny snapped her fingers in front of my face. "Hel-loooo. Where'd you go?"

I blinked. "Sorry. I guess I'm tired too."

"It's been a long week," she confirmed.

"My week's not over. I'm going to the show tonight. I want to see how everything runs for an event."

"Social Proof? They're good. I saw them last year."

"Yeah, about that. How come you didn't tell me there was an event team? I assumed I was going to be running around like a chicken with my head cut off, but apparently, we have a whole crew."

She paled. "I'm so sorry. With the fundraiser planning and my impending date, it totally slipped my mind. Suzette never wanted to be involved. She had me handle everything. I guess I never gave it a second thought."

"No worries. I get it, things have been crazy. Any word from Ariel Fox's manager yet?"

"Not a word." She sighed. "I've left like four messages."

I frowned. "That sucks. I'm going to call her myself. They can't ignore us forever."

"Actually, they can."

"Stop being a pessimist." I waved a hand at her. "I need to at least book her for a few shows, but a residency would help secure my position here."

"You don't need to worry about job security. You've accomplished more in two weeks than Suzette did in months. Plus, I noticed Mr. Broody Pants hasn't been so grumpy lately. You must be doing something right."

The conversation was veering into dangerous territory, so I made a quick detour. "I'm sure that has nothing to do with me. He's probably getting laid." I wanted to smack myself before the words finished falling from my lips. It was so stupid. Why would I say that about my boss?

"He gets laid plenty," Penny said. "I've heard he has a way with the ladies, though I haven't personally seen it. I mean, he's hot, but he's kind of a big dick. But who knows, maybe he *has* a big dick and that's what attracts the women."

I choked on my Diet Coke and held a hand over my mouth to keep it from spraying all over my desk. Swallowing it down, I coughed as the bubbles burned my throat. If only she knew how true her words were. "Sorry. Wrong pipe." I banged on my chest with the heel of my hand. "So, what are you wearing on your date?" Focusing back on Penny was my only option. I didn't think I could handle another comment about Trent's dick.

She put a finger to her lips. "I'm not sure. Nothing in my closet screams French cuisine."

"Come on, it's time to go shopping," I said as I grabbed my purse from the desk drawer. "I saw the perfect dress for you in one of the boutiques downstairs. My treat for all the extra help you've given me." I hauled her out of the chair and toward the door. "You're going to look fabulous."

One crisis averted. I hoped I could survive the rest of the night with a little more grace.

I met Trent in the lobby at exactly seven o'clock. He looked utterly delicious in dark jeans and a black button-up shirt. He'd left it untucked and had the sleeves rolled up, showing off his muscular forearms and a hint of that tattoo I'd yet to identify. This was the first time I'd seen him in something other than a suit, and I completely approved. Casual Trent was just as hot as Office Trent.

He let out a low whistle when he saw me. I did a spin to give him a view of the low-cut back on my silver tank. I'd paired it with cropped jeans and a pair of strappy, silver heels. "You like?"

He pulled me by the hand and pecked me on the cheek, then eyed me from head to toe. "You look gorgeous."

I scanned the area to see if anyone was watching us, but everyone was busy doing their own thing. "You don't look so bad yourself. I was starting to wonder if you owned anything other than suits."

"I do, indeed." He pulled a laminated badge from his back pocket and handed it to me. "This is your backstage pass for all events. We keep security tight, but you can go anywhere with that."

"Gianna Romano, Director of Entertainment and Events," I read aloud. "So, it's official now?"

"It was official the minute I said it." Trent took the pass from me and hung the lanyard around my neck.

I giggled. I wasn't much of a giggler, but I couldn't help myself. "Has anyone ever told you you're bossy?"

His mouth quirked up on one side. "A time or two." He held out his arm for me. "Are you ready for your first Vegas show?"

"Ready as I'll ever be." I looped my arm through his. "I've never been backstage for a concert before."

"Then you're in for a treat. Best seats in the house." He led me through the back hallways to two huge black doors. A big, beefy guy stood guard with his arms crossed. "Hey, Mason."

He dropped the tough guy persona I was sure he had no problem backing up and smiled at Trent. "Hey, boss man." Mason held his fist out for Trent to bump. "Long time no see. Who's your lady friend?"

"Gia, Mason. Mason, this is Miss Gia Romano, our new director of entertainment and events."

Mason took my small hand in his big paw with the gentleness of a teddy bear. "Nice to meet you, Miss Romano."

"Likewise. And it's Gia."

"I was hoping you could take a few minutes to show Gia around and introduce her to the crew," Trent said.

"Sure thing, boss." Mason spoke into his walkie, "Jasper, need you to take my place for a few."

Within minutes, Jasper appeared, and introductions were made. He was as big as Mason, if not bigger. Mystique didn't mess around when it came to security. Mason held the door open for us. "After you."

I slipped inside with Trent and was hit with a sense of urgency. People hustled around the huge space like bees in a hive. Some had clipboards, others pushed equipment around, and still others spoke into mics attached to their shirts. Everyone was busy getting things in order for tonight's show.

One woman stood out from the rest. Forty-something, if I had to guess, a clipboard in hand, and a headset perched atop her curly, blond hair pulled into a ponytail. She barked out orders and directed the crew. "Who is she?"

"That's Scarlet. She's our fairy godmother; makes the magic happen. Nothing goes down back here without her knowledge. She's also the liaison between the hotel and the performers."

"Introduce me?" It was nice to see another woman in a position of authority. Woman power and all that. I already liked Scarlet.

"Sure thing."

We talked to Scarlet briefly. She was a busy woman, and I didn't want to interrupt, but I scheduled a meeting with her for next week. She knew all the ins and outs of the business and I hoped she'd be able to help me with Ariel Fox.

Before we knew it, the show was ready to start. Trent moved us into the wings, out of the way of the road crew and out of sight from the audience. The packed theater buzzed with energy. You could literally feel it coming off the crowd in waves.

The lights went down, and everyone went crazy with anticipation. Trent wrapped his arms around me from behind and rested them on my hips. "Are you ready for this?" he whispered in my ear.

I nodded furiously. "So ready."

A single drumbeat from the stage, slow and steady. The rhythm of a guitar joined the beat, and then a second guitar. A deep baritone voice began right as the stage lit up and the crowd went wild.

My hips swayed and my chest thumped with every beat of the drums. I couldn't just hear the music, I felt it coursing through my body. It became a part of me.

About halfway through the set, Trent whispered in my ear, "Are you trying to drive me crazy?"

Goose bumps ran down my spine. "Just enjoying the show."

"So am I."

"This is phenomenal."

"I'm not talking about the music. For two weeks you've been teasing me and now you're shaking your hips against my junk."

I winced at him, scolding myself for my carelessness. I'd set boundaries and my hips were sending the wrong message. "I wasn't trying to tease you, I just got lost in the music." The show was great, but I wanted to find out what else this man had in store for me. Tonight was supposed to be about getting to know each other. "You wanna get out of here?"

He chuckled. "Only if you're ready."

The look in his chocolate-brown eyes told me he was more than ready. "I've done my due diligence. What else you got?"

Trent groaned. "So much more, sweetheart. So much."

My panties flooded from the man who was offering more than I was willing to give. Yet. I didn't want to fuck up my job, but the man holding my hips was too tempting for his own good. He'd have to wait until I decided if he was worth the risk. "I wanna see more than the inside of a hotel room."

"Not even on my mind," he lied as he pressed his cock into the small of my back. "I'm going to make tonight a night you'll never forget."

"Show me what you've got," I flirted. "I wanna live dangerously."

"Careful what you wish for." Trent grabbed my hand and dragged me through the throng of people backstage. I giggled as I ran in my heels down the winding corridors of Mystique I never knew existed. We exited the venue through a side door and proceeded down a deserted path to the crowded sidewalk of the Strip.

There was so much to take in—couples walking arm in arm, drag queens drumming up business for their shows, lights flashing and demanding attention. My knowledge of the Strip was limited. Since I'd been here, I'd experienced it through the window of my new living quarters, seeing it from afar but not being immersed in the sights and sounds.

"Where are we going?"

"Everywhere. No more naive girl from Waukegan. You need to live!"

I loved his enthusiasm. It was a lot to absorb as we weaved in and out of tourists. Finally, he stopped and pulled me in front of him, wrapping his arms around my waist. "This is a must-see." Trent pushed me against the railing, shielding me from behind.

I looked over the small pond in front of a grand hotel. "What am I looking at?"

"Just wait."

Minutes ticked by and I wasn't sure what I was supposed to look at. Music played and the magic began. Water danced in front of me in a carefully choreographed display of lights and sound. I was transfixed by the fountains as they sprayed water in perfect harmony with the music. "This is the Bellagio?"

"It is. What do you think?"

"Wow. It's better than YouTube."

He watched me watch the fountains. "Nothing is better than the real thing. This is only the beginning."

After the fantastic water display, we walked hand in hand down the Strip. He led me past the Eiffel Tower, roller coasters, and street performers. It truly was an adult playground. Too much and not enough all at the same time. An overload of the senses that made you afraid you might miss something if you blinked.

Placing his palm on my lower back, Trent led me past huge statues of lions guarding the entrance of another casino. It was extravagant, as if everything was dipped in gold. "What are we doing here?"

"You'll see," Trent said as he led me through the lobby and onto the casino floor. The dinging of the slot machines overwhelmed me from every side. "Pick one."

There were so many. A sea of spinning reels revealing diamonds, cherries, lucky sevens, and any other image you could think of. "I don't know how to choose."

"My mom always says the machine picks you. Take a deep breath and close your eyes." I did as he said, and Trent turned me in a circle. "Now open your eyes. Which machine calls to you?"

I took a tentative step forward, focusing on a slot machine in the far corner. Trent followed my lead and slipped a hundred dollar bill into the bandit like it was nothing. "I can't spend your money."

"Sure you can. It's a date and I can afford it. You haven't even let me buy you dinner." He nodded toward the machine. "Pull the handle."

I bit my lip in anticipation. It seemed like a waste of money, but I couldn't fight the urge to give it a try. "You're sure?"

He gave me a pointed look and placed my hand on the lever. "I'm positive."

It was five dollars a spin. Money that would be better spent on anything else. I pushed away the inner voice of my parents and pulled down. The reels spun quickly, landing on a double bar, a seven, and a blank. I shrugged, feeling guilty for wasting Trent's money.

He chuckled. "I'd have been surprised if you won anything on the first try." Leaning over me, he tapped the credit button three times. "Try again."

I gulped. "That's fifteen dollars."

He rolled his eyes and put my hand back on the lever. "Pull."

The wheels spun again and the pit in my stomach grew. It was one thing wasting my own money, but it was something else entirely to waste his. I watched intently as the reels stopped one by one, a bar, another bar, and... a cherry. My heart sank. How could people put their hard-earned money into these machines day after day? A tiny ding grabbed my attention. "What happened?"

Trent smirked at me. "You won your money back."

"Your money," I corrected. "So, it's what? Like a free spin?"

"That's how they keep you here. Gives you a little taste of success. Can you feel it?"

I nodded.

"Go ahead. Pull it again. You know you want to."

I did want to do it again. A rush of adrenaline coursed through my veins. I copied Trent and tapped the credit button three times. "Here goes nothing." With a pull of the handle the reels spun again. Three double bars clicked into place and the machine dinged longer than before, giving me thirty credits. I quickly did the math. "A hundred fifty?"

"Looks like it's your lucky night."

"I should stop."

"No. You should keep going. You'll know when to stop."

"Do you want to play?"

Trent shook his head at me with a predatory glint in his eyes. "I'm enjoying watching you."

"Is this turning you on?"

"Immensely."

I giggled. "You're a strange one." I began mixing up my bets, sometimes winning a bit and sometimes losing. Every time the machine dinged it was like another shot of adrenaline straight to the heart. It was easy to see how people became so addicted. When I'd doubled Trent's initial investment, I cashed out and held up the slip that was spat out. "Drinks on me?"

"Absolutely." Trent pulled the slip from between my fingers and led us to the cashier. After cashing out, we sat at the bar and ordered. "Are you hungry?"

"I grabbed a burger with Claude before the concert, but I could eat." I held up my cosmo. "Something to soak this up. A corn dog?"

Trent nearly spits his scotch on the bar top. "We're in a city where you can literally get anything, and you want carnival food?"

"I'm a midwestern girl. I don't need fancy. I need sustenance."

"You are something else, Gia Romano. A complete and utter enigma."

I quirked a brow at him. "That a problem for you?"

"Not at all. It's refreshing."

126

Chapter 20
Trent

I hadn't had a corn dog since college, and for the life of me I couldn't figure out why. Being with Gia took me back to a time when life was simpler. That first year of college was the best. No one knew who I was or had any expectations of me. I was a guy living life to the fullest. A pretty girl wrapped in my arms, a beer in my hand, and the world at my fingertips.

Somewhere along the way, I forgot how to live. I'd been so focused on success and proving myself, I'd been existing instead of living. I rarely laughed, nights out were limited, and sex was functional. Don't get me wrong, I loved sex, but I was emotionally unattached. I'd been one and done for years. After Morgan wiped me out, my faith in women went down the tubes. I swore I'd never put myself in that position again.

Which was why my visceral response to Gia threw me off-kilter. She evoked emotions I'd buried so long ago I barely recognized them anymore. She made me laugh and want more than the meager life I'd been living. For the first time in forever, I wanted more than one night.

I handed her the corn dog from the street vendor and the expression on her face over such a simple thing had me shaking my head.

"What?" she asked through a mouthful of hot dog and fried batter.

"You. That's all."

"Well," she said, holding a hand over her mouth as she chewed, "I don't know if that's a good thing or a bad thing."

"It's a good thing. A very good thing. Come on." I tugged on her hand as we walked and finished our greasy, late-night snack. "I want to show you something."

"There's more?" Gia tossed her empty stick and napkin into a garbage can. "I feel like I could spend weeks here and not see everything."

I loved watching her face light up and the astonishment shining in her blue eyes. This city was home to me, but to her it was a mystical adventure. "Good thing you've got an expert tour guide." I wrapped my arm around her shoulders and pulled her into my chest, pecking a kiss to her temple. The light floral scent of her perfume invaded my senses and made my head swim. I was in deep with this woman, and I'd barely scratched the surface of who she was or what we could be. That I was even thinking of a future still took my breath away. Caught me by surprise and sent me sideways.

Reaching our destination, I paid the attendant for two tickets and led Gia to the silver doors that slid open. We stepped into the elevator and Gia tentatively placed her hand on the glass wall that separated us from the city lights. I stepped behind her and pressed my hand atop hers, then kissed along the length of her neck. "Trent," she whispered. "Someone will see…" her words were cut off by the jerk of the elevator lifting. She trembled. "I feel like we're flying, floating in midair. It's spectacular and terrifying." We rose above the hustle and bustle, leaving the chaos below.

It was as if I was seeing the city for the first time, through her eyes, and it was indeed spectacular. "I won't let anything happen to you."

Gia turned her head and smiled up at me from where I towered over her. "Big promises," she said, repeating the words she'd said our first night together.

My fingers twined with hers on the glass. "I kept my promise then and I intend to keep it now."

Her cheeks flushed, no doubt remembering the things we did that night, same as I was doing. Something about this woman had me coming apart.

Wanting things I had no business wanting. Before I had a chance to ponder it further, the car slid to a stop and the doors opened behind us. I led her out to the open-air viewing deck.

She gripped the railing and threw her head back. The wind caught the ends of her hair and tossed it around her beautiful face as she breathed in the crisp night air. "It's gorgeous," she gasped.

I stepped back and looked at her. Red hair blowing in the breeze. A shimmery tank draped low in the back, exposing milky-white perfection inked with pink cherry blossoms that danced across her skin. Hips Shakira would be jealous of, and long legs clad in denim. "Definitely gorgeous."

Gia playfully slapped my shoulder. "I'm talking about the view, you goofball."

"So am I."

"Are you objectifying me, Mr. Dorsey?"

"Absolutely. In the very best way." I caged her against the rail with my arms. "You ready to go home? I want some alone time with you."

"We've been alone all night." She smiled as she teased me.

I rolled my eyes at her. "*Alone* alone time. I don't want to share you with ten thousand people."

"We're not having sex," she reiterated the conditions from two days ago.

"I'm aware." Although I knew her terms, my dick hadn't gotten the memo. He was on board for a night of dirty depravity. "We won't do anything you don't want to do." It was the gentlemanly thing to say, even if I didn't feel very gentlemanly. Sex was definitely at the forefront of my mind.

Gia turned and wrapped her arms around my waist. "Let's go."

We leisurely walked back to Mystique, our hands twined together as if it were the most natural thing in the world. When we approached the entrance, she stopped and swung our arms between us. "Thank you for tonight. I had a wonderful time. And yes, you are an impressive tour guide."

She was crazy if she thought our night was ending this way. "I'll walk you in."

She glanced at the glass doors and back at me. "I don't think that's a good idea."

I pressed a finger to her lips. "With my dad in Hawaii and Hunter in Albuquerque, we don't have to hide." I intended to use these few weeks to my advantage.

She bit her lip. "No sex."

I crossed myself even though I hadn't been to church since my communion. "Not even on my mind." We headed to the elevator, and I pushed the button for the top floor.

Gia looked at the panel and then focused on me. "Do you live in the hotel too?"

It was then I knew I fucked up. "No."

She pressed the six and gave me a death glare. "What's on the top floor, Trent?"

I stood silent, not willing to give her an answer to the question that was about to end this night in a less than spectacular way.

"Does Brett live here?"

"No."

"What's on the top floor, Trent?" she asks accusingly.

Again, I had no answer. Not one that would satisfy her. "Nothing. I pushed the wrong button is all."

I could tell when the pieces came together. "That's where you took me that first night. It's your fuck pad, isn't it?" She shook her head. "And here I thought you were actually starting to like me. But I'm just another one of your conquests."

I cringed. "It's not like that. I do like you. I wasn't thinking."

She held up a hand to stop my lame explanation. "I don't need to hear anymore." The elevator dinged, opening on her floor. She stepped out and held the door with one hand. "Thank you for tonight. I had a great time. I'll see you Monday."

"Gia…" I went to follow her, but she released the door, and it closed in my face. *Fuuuuck!* The elevator descended as I leaned back against the wall berating myself. After what Brett and I did, combined with Hunter's outright propositioning, I couldn't blame her for being upset. I stepped out into the

130

crowded lobby as an entire bachelor party stumbled in, laughing and joking from their night out on the town. Their easy, carefree behavior made me more pissed at myself. I agreed to no sex and then disrespected her by pushing that damn button.

How could I have been so stupid?

Chapter 21

Gia

How could I have been so stupid?

I slipped my key card into the lock and pressed my back against the door as it closed behind me. I almost fell for it. The convincing act he put on. I thought it was real.

He was good, I'd give him that. I replayed our evening, trying to figure out what I'd missed. The way he held my hips as we swayed to the music. The subtle hand on my lower back. The intimate hand-holding. The gentle kisses on my neck.

I thought he cared about me, but it was all an act. I should have known his intent was to get me back into bed. I wasn't against sleeping with him again, but I wanted it to mean something. I didn't want to be just another fuck.

I should have followed my instincts and refused to go out with him. Put a hard line between us. He was my boss, and he had a reputation for being a ladies' man. Why did I think I would be any different than the dozens of women that came before me? I couldn't lie, I had a great time wandering around the city with him. It felt like we were building something.

But it was a lie.

My phone buzzed in my purse. It could only be one person texting me at two in the morning and I didn't have the heart to listen to any more of his lies. I put my phone on the charger and went to bed. I had the rest of the weekend to rebuild my armor against Trent.

Starting Monday, we'd be back to business only.

With last night playing on repeat, I barely got any sleep and now the pounding in my head wouldn't go away. I only had one drink, yet the constant beat, beat, beat wouldn't stop. The light coming through the partially closed drapes nearly blinded me and the pounding began again, only this time I realized it wasn't in my head but coming from the front room.

I dragged myself out of bed, pulled on a robe, and cracked the door. A food cart covered in silver trays was set outside. "I didn't order any food. You have the wrong room." I yawned, ready to go back to sleep.

"It's the right room."

You've got to be kidding. I opened the door fully. "You can leave the cart and see yourself out." I headed to the bathroom and locked myself inside. There was no way I was getting more sleep this morning, so I brushed my teeth, threw my hair up in a ponytail, and washed my face.

The smell of bacon lured me out, only to find Trent still in my room, setting the dishes on the table with a vase of beautiful wildflowers. "What is all this?"

"It's an apology. I fucked up last night." He removed the silver lids and placed them on the empty cart. "I didn't know what you liked, so I got a little bit of everything."

I blew out a breath in frustration. "It's not necessary. Last night was what it was. I had fun, but I think it's better if we cut our losses now. I can't be another one of your flings. I don't do casual."

Trent pulled out a chair for me. "At least have breakfast."

"Fine." I sat and scooted my chair in. "You might as well join me. There's enough food here to feed a third-world country." I scooped scrambled eggs, bacon, and half a waffle onto my plate. No need to let good food go to waste.

He pulled up another chair and filled his plate. "I'd like to renegotiate your terms."

I dropped my fork, letting it clatter on my plate. "This isn't a business deal. I'm not another client who can be manipulated."

"I'm not trying to manipulate you." He held up a hand to stop my retort. "I know it seemed that way last night, but I really wasn't. It was an involuntary response."

I laughed at his absurdity. "So, your finger *involuntarily* hit the button to your fuck pad after I specifically said no sex?"

He shook his head. "That sounds terrible."

"It does, but they're your words, not mine." I cut off a chunk of waffle drenched in syrup and stuffed it in my mouth, mostly to keep myself from saying what was really on my mind. That he was a manwhoring, presumptuous asshole.

Trent finished chewing his eggs. "I'm not going to lie. I did want to have sex with you, because you're sexy as fuck, but... I wasn't trying to manipulate you into something you weren't ready for. I enjoyed our evening and would have been satisfied with kissing. Last night was the first actual date I've had in a long time that didn't take place in the bedroom. My old habits kicked in and I'm sorry. I haven't had a relationship in a while. The last time I got burned, so I'm a bit out of practice."

I appreciated his honesty, but I was still mad. "This ought to be good. Please tell me how the great Trent Dorsey got taken advantage of by a woman."

"I'd really rather not rehash it."

"If you want me to entertain renegotiating, then I'm going to need the fine print. It's Business 101."

He groaned. "Why do you have to be beautiful *and* smart?"

I waved a piece of bacon at him. "Flattery will only get you so far. Spill the tea." Despite being pissed about his misstep last night, I was curious.

Trent grabbed the pitcher of orange juice and poured a glass for each of us, setting mine in front of me. "When I was twenty-five, I dated a dancer. I met her in the club and fell for her immediately."

"A stripper?"

"An exotic dancer who, yes, worked in a gentlemen's club. Don't be judgy."

I mocked zipping my lips and waited for him to continue.

"Anyway, we dated for a while and when she needed a place to stay, I didn't hesitate to let her move in with me. Two weeks later, she disappeared with my grandfather's watch, my wallet, and the cash in my bank account. Cleaned me out."

My eyebrows rose. "Well, that sucks."

"To put it mildly. Since then, I've had trust issues."

"Hence, no relationships."

He gave a curt nod.

I took a sip of my juice and set the glass back on the table. "Thank you for sharing that with me." I stared at the tattoo on his arm that mystified me for weeks and ran my finger over the ink. It was a snake wrapped around a dagger, fangs biting into an apple. "What does this mean to you?"

"Temptation. It's always been my downfall and I've paid the price. I didn't want to put myself in that position again. No woman was worth the risk." Reaching for my hand, Trent folded our fingers together. "Until you."

"Why me?"

"There's something about you I can't resist. I knew that first night if I ever saw you again it would be game over for me. It was supposed to be one night. Then you showed up in the conference room and blew my self-control to shit. I didn't want to like you. I didn't want you to be good at your job. And I sure as hell didn't want you to be so damn gorgeous."

"I'm sorry?" What else was I supposed to say to him. "If it helps, I didn't want to like you either."

"I wanted you to hate me."

"Is that why you were an arrogant jerk?"

135

"Yes, but I'm done with that. I want to give this a try. I can't promise you a relationship, but it won't be a fling."

"Terms of negotiation… I'm never going back to that room and as long as we're giving this a try, neither are you. There won't be anyone else."

"Terms accepted. Come here." He pulled me onto his lap and cradled my face in his hand. "I didn't get to give you a good-night kiss."

Staring into his dark-chocolate eyes, I was hypnotized just like I'd been that first night. "What are you waiting for?" I whispered.

"Not a damn thing." He pressed his lips to mine in a possessive kiss that made my toes tingle and my heart race. I wrapped my arms around his neck and pulled him closer. His tongue ran along the seam of my lips, begging for entrance. There was no denying the chemistry between us. I opened willingly, letting his tongue tangle with mine. We devoured each other with a passion I hadn't felt in years. Both of us were breathing heavily when he pulled away. "Goddamn, you're perfect."

"I like the kissing. Why are you stopping?"

Trent pressed his forehead against mine. "I knew you were trouble from the moment I set my eyes on you. If I don't stop now, I'm not going to, and it will ruin all my planning." He picked up a piece of bacon and held it to my lips. "Finish your breakfast and then get dressed. I'm taking you sightseeing."

Moving to my own seat, I finished the food on my plate and nodded to the vase. "Thank you for the flowers. That was sweet of you."

"You're welcome. Am I forgiven?"

"Yes."

The man made my head swim, but I couldn't resist him either.

Chapter 22
Trent

I spent the day showing Gia the sights of Las Vegas off the Strip. We went to the Hoover Dam, then hiked through the Red Rock Canyon. It'd been years since I hiked and even though I worked out several times a week, my muscles were tired. "Let's take a break," I said as we approached a huge boulder that overlooked the canyon.

Gia sat on the edge with her legs dangling. "This is an amazing view." She took out her phone and snapped a few pictures. "I've got to send these to my sister. She's going to be jealous."

I knew she had a sister from the research Tom did, but beyond the basics, I didn't know shit about the woman sitting next to me. "Tell me about your sister," I said as I handed her a water bottle from my backpack.

She held her phone up and took another picture. "Her name is Bianca and she's two years older than me." Gia took a long gulp of water and wiped her mouth with the back of her hand. "We used to be close when we were younger, but she got married young and has three kids. Everyone expected me to follow in her footsteps."

"So you got married?"

She looked out over the canyon. "I did. John and I grew up across the street from each other and were best friends since the time we were six. It was assumed we would always be together, so when I graduated college, we got married."

"Wow. You never dated anyone else?"

She wobbled her head back and forth. "I went on some dates in high school and college, but nothing ever stuck, you know? It always felt like cheating. Even though we weren't an official couple, John and I were soul mates."

"Why didn't it work?"

Gia let out a big sigh. "Part of me will always love him, but we wanted different things. He wanted the small-town life with a barefoot wife and half a dozen kids. I wanted the city life and a career where I wore expensive shoes. Kids eventually, but not now. I wanted to live first. I couldn't keep having the same conversation over and over again, so I filed for divorce and moved back home. Nobody understood, sometimes not even me."

"Do you regret it? Getting divorced?" I wanted this to work with her, but not if she was wallowing in regret and in love with another man.

"I don't regret getting divorced. What I regret is hurting my best friend. We should have never gotten married in the first place."

"If he really cares about you, he'll forgive you."

She gave a self-deprecating laugh. "That's the kicker. He already did." She shrugged. "John's a good guy. It's my family that's having a hard time accepting it."

I wrapped my arm around her shoulders and pulled her into my side. It wasn't regret she felt, it was guilt. "There's nothing wrong with chasing your dreams."

"I want to prove them wrong. If I fail, it'll validate every person who doubted me."

I lifted her chin. "You're not going to fail. I believe in you."

Her lips turned up. "Thank you."

I closed the gap between us and pressed a gentle kiss to her soft lips. "You're welcome. What do you say we grab an early dinner? I know a good steak place."

"That would be perfect. I'm starving again." She looked down at her shorts and tank top. "I'm not exactly dressed for dinner."

"It's casual. I promise." I stood and reached for Gia's hand, pulling her to her feet. Lacing our fingers together, our arms swung between us on the walk back to my Audi.

We sat on the patio of a favorite local restaurant. Over steak and shrimp, I told her about growing up in Vegas and explained my complicated relationship with Hunter. She told me more about her family and growing up outside of Chicago. The conversation flowed naturally between us with easy laughter and familiarity. Eventually, it rolled back to our precarious situation.

Gia sipped her Diet Coke. "So, how long is Hunter gone?"

I stabbed another shrimp with my fork. "A month and I'm going to enjoy the reprieve. He's been all up in my shit ever since my father gave me the ultimatum. My mom and dad won't be back until just before the fundraiser."

"You shouldn't tell Brett we've been hanging out," she said.

I cocked an eyebrow. "Hanging out?"

She shrugged a shoulder. "Let's be honest. Neither one of us knows where this is going yet. And until we figure it out, I'd prefer no one knows."

I understood her reasoning, but I'd shared a lot more than secrets with Brett over the years. "He won't say anything."

"You sure about that?"

"Positive. And he's certainly not going to tell Hunter or my dad."

"I'm more concerned about Penny."

That didn't make any sense. "I don't understand."

She bowed her head and giggled into her fist. "I guess he really is a vault."

"Care to fill me in?" There was a joke there somewhere, but I was missing it.

She held up a hand and waved it as she continued to laugh. "I can't…"

"So help me, Gianna, if you don't tell me right now, I'll…" *I would what?* There was no threat I could make I'd be willing to carry out. "Just tell me."

"Penny and Brett went on a date last night. He took her to some fancy French place."

"Huh?"

Gia giggled again. "You really didn't know?"

I shook my head. "That sneaky little bastard."

She shrugged as she took another bite of her steak. "Anyway, if it went well, then he'd probably tell Penny about us. I trust her, but until we know what this is, we don't need everyone knowing our business."

"Agreed." I felt a pang of betrayal by Brett, but then again, I hadn't filled him in on my weekend plans either. I knew he had a thing for her, I just didn't think he'd act on it. "Does Penny know about what happened between the three of us?"

"Hell no! I'd never tell her. She really likes him, and it would break her heart. She's got enough confidence issues as it is. Even if it doesn't work out with them, it's a hard no."

I smiled at her. "You're a good friend. Something tells me you're loyal to a fault."

"I am. My circle is small, but once you're in, I'd do about anything for you."

"Am I in your circle?" I teased.

She waved her hand back and forth. "You're on the fringe. It takes more than waffles and flowers to get inside the circle."

I held up a finger. "And bacon. Bacon has got to count for something."

"Bonus points, for sure." She laughed. "But bacon will only take you so far."

Although I wanted her to let me in, I understood her hesitancy. I was a dick from the first day she stepped into my office. Her walls were high, but not higher than mine. I wanted to fully trust her, but I wasn't in any hurry to take her back to my own apartment. Trust needed to be earned and we were still getting to know each other. "What do you want to do tonight?"

Gia raised her eyebrows. "You're not sick of me yet?"

"Not in the least. Are you sick of me?"

"Hmmm. Well, you did wake me up this morning..."

"But I brought bacon," I pointed out.

"Very true. And you have given me the grand tour of Vegas without wearing on my nerves completely." She stopped to take a sip and smiled at me. "I suppose I can handle a bit more time with you."

I growled with lust. This girl had me unraveling from both ends. I couldn't remember the last time I'd begged a woman to spend time with me. "The tour is not complete. I still have more I want to show you." In particular, my throbbing cock inside her pussy.

"Easy, killer. I was thinking more of Netflix and chill after a hot shower."

Now I was picturing her naked in the shower, tits pressed against the tile and ass in the air. My dick swelled even more at the idea of taking her from behind with bubbles sliding off her voluptuous curves. "I'm in for a shower."

"Alone. I'm going to be showering alone, but you're welcome to come by after."

"Fine," I huffed. "Netflix and chill it is."

I paid for our meal and drove her back to Mystique. She hopped out without so much as a peck on the cheek. Leaning through the window, she wiggled her fingers at me. "Thank you for another great day. I'll see you in a couple hours. Toodles."

Her shorts-clad ass swayed and disappeared through the sliding doors, my view blocked by the eager valet moving toward my open window. "Staying, Mr. Dorsey?"

I peered around him, trying to get one more glimpse of Gia, but she was long gone. "I'll be back." Shifting into gear, I hightailed it to my own apartment.

She may have eluded me again, but I was a persistent motherfucker.

"What's in the bags?" she asked while holding the door open for me.

I pushed past her and set my purchases on the small table. "Everything we need for a night in." She tried peeking in the bags, but I pulled them away. "Patience, grasshopper."

Gia looked adorable in casual cotton shorts and a plain black tank. Her ample breasts looked phenomenal and her legs… ugh… long and toned. Her makeup was subtle, and her hair braided down her back. I liked that she didn't try too hard. She was as beautiful in her natural state as when she was fully done up.

"What?" she asked

"Huh?"

"You're staring at me."

I shook my head. "Sorry. You should try not looking so tempting."

Gia rolled her eyes. "You're ridiculous." She motioned to the table. "The bags, Casanova."

"Right." I pulled out a few packages of microwave popcorn, thankful this dinky room even had a microwave. "Option one." I dumped the rest of the bag on the table, spilling out an assortment of candy. "Option two." Moving to the other bag, I pulled out all the ingredients for sundaes—vanilla and chocolate ice cream, chocolate syrup, cherries, sprinkles, and whipped cream. "Option three. And to wash it all down…" I opened the last bag and set the contents on the table. "We have an assortment to select from… soda, iced tea, or wine."

Gia picked up the bottle of wine and inspected it. "This looks fancy."

It was four hundred dollars for the bottle and worth every penny. "It's not fancy," I lied.

"Hmmm." She set the bottle back on the table. "Well, it's not Boone's Farm, so that's fancy in my book." Gia surveyed the table full of snacks. "Would you be upset if we waited a bit before digging into all this?"

"Not at all. I probably went a bit overboard." I put the ice cream in the freezer and the wine in the fridge to chill. I was hoping a glass of wine would loosen her up, but the night was young and as much as I was ready to get her back in bed again, letting her take her time was more important. I already knew what I wanted, but it needed to be her choice.

"A bit overboard, but the sentiment is sweet." She moved to the small couch that was barely big enough for the two of us and tapped the seat next to her. "Any requests?"

I plopped down next to her, close but not too close, tossing the throw pillow aside. "I mostly watch sports and news, so whatever you want is fine."

Gia pulled her legs up on the couch and crossed them in front of her. The innocent action had my fingers twitching with the need to touch her creamy, smooth skin. She scrolled through the options on Netflix, but I didn't pay a bit of attention to what was on the screen. I'd rather watch her. "There's a new thriller trending. Want to try it?"

It'd been forever since I'd done anything as mundane as watching a movie with a woman, but for her, I'd watch paint dry if she asked me to. "A thriller sounds perfect."

Gia held up a finger. "Hold on a minute." She jumped up and disappeared into her bedroom, returning with a leopard-print blanket. "You wanna share it with me?"

I chuckled. There was no way this was the same woman who gave me hell in the office. The two sides of her were like completely different people and I found both of them just as appealing. "No thanks. I'm good."

She shrugged. "Suit yourself." Gia curled up on the couch and tossed the blanket over her legs.

I patted my chest and held out my arm. "Come here. Most comfortable seat in the house."

She scooted the couple of inches and leaned into me, resting her head on my chest while I wrapped my arm around her. "Hmm. This is pretty cozy. Maybe we *should* get the snacks before starting the movie."

"Pick your poison and I'll get it."

"Popcorn and wine." She scrunched up her nose. "Is that strange?"

"Totally strange, but perfectly acceptable." I unwrapped myself from around her and headed to the tiny kitchen. "Why don't you go ahead and get our movie queued up?" I tossed the popcorn in the microwave for two minutes and opened the cupboard in search of something to dump it into. The kitchen was surprisingly well stocked for temporary living quarters, and

I easily found a large glass bowl and two wineglasses while the corn popped. Armed with our snack and wine, I set everything on the small coffee table, pulled it closer to the couch, and reclaimed my seat. Gia curled into my side with remote in hand. "Are you ready now?"

Gia gazed up at me through long lashes. "Blanket, popcorn, wine, and you... what more could a girl ask for?" She reached for one of the glasses and took a small sip. "Wow! This is good. Really good," she said, taking a more generous gulp.

"Nothing but the best for you." I kissed her temple and enjoyed the warmth of having her in my arms.

"Thank you." She pressed play and the screen came to life.

We watched in amicable silence, munching on popcorn and sipping four-hundred-dollar wine. The room dimmed as the sun set, casting Gia's features in a warm glow from the television. I couldn't keep my eyes off her long lashes, high cheekbones, and pouty lips.

"You're staring at me again," she said without looking away from the screen.

"I can't help it. You're too damn beautiful."

Gia looked up at me with her ocean-blue eyes. "Yeah?" she whispered.

"Yeah. I'm gonna kiss you now."

"Then kiss me."

It was all the permission I needed to seize her lips with mine, trying my damnedest to be gentle when all I wanted to do was consume her. My tongue ran along the seam of her luscious lips, begging for entrance. Once she complied, it was game over. I unleashed everything I'd been holding back for the last few weeks. I wanted this woman more tonight than I did the first time we met, but instead of being a shared appetizer, I wanted her as my full five-course dinner. I'd never been so hungry in my life.

My hands skimmed her body, grazing the sides of her tits. She moaned as her fingers worked the buttons on my shirt and slipped inside. I lifted her to straddle my lap, pressing her center against the hard-on trapped inside my jeans. She felt too good.

Too soft.

Too warm.

144

Too tempting.

"Tell me to stop." Instead, she lifted her arms in invitation. I slowly lifted her shirt up and off, baring her gorgeous breasts clad in a lacy black bra. "So beautiful." With one arm around her waist and the other supporting her neck, I leaned her back and peppered kisses along her generous mounds of exposed flesh.

"Don't stop." Reaching behind her, she released the clasp of her bra and eased the straps down her shoulders, teasing me and testing my patience. I grabbed the lacy material with my teeth and ripped it away from her body with a growl. She giggled at my antics, thrusting her tits toward my face.

I spit the lace to the side. "Careful, sweetheart. You don't know what you're unleashing."

"I have an idea and I'm not afraid."

That was it. The approval I'd been seeking. Capturing one perfect nipple with my lips, I suckled the tip, laved it with my tongue, and pulled it deeper into my mouth. Giving her other tit the same attention, I worshipped them with all the care they deserved.

Gia ran her hands through my hair, scraping her nails along my scalp and sending tingles down my spine. She rocked her pussy against my erection, molding herself around it and making it even harder. This woman made me crazy with lust and desire. I grabbed her hips. "Stop wiggling or you'll make me come like a fifteen-year-old."

"Maybe that's my intention."

"You're trouble." I lightly bit her shoulder as a warning.

"Trent?" she gasped.

"Yes?"

"Take me to bed."

Fuck… finally!

Chapter 23
Gia

Trent growled as he stood, taking me with him. I wrapped my legs around his waist, locking my ankles behind his back. He carried me to the bedroom and laid me in the middle of the bed. The wine I drank made me loose and giddy, enough buzz to take away my inhibitions, but not so much as to take away my senses.

I sat up on my elbows and watched in the dim light as he finished unbuttoning his shirt from the bottom up and shrugged it off his shoulders, exposing his toned chest and tight abs. "You look like you want to eat me alive," I teased.

"Eating your pussy is definitely on my list." He tugged me by the ankles and pulled me to the edge of the bed. "I've been thinking about this since the day you walked into my office."

With his fingers tucked into the waist of my shorts, I lifted a foot and braced it against his chest, pushing myself back to center. "Wait."

He froze. "You're killing me, sweetheart."

Indecision filled my head. I had a million thoughts I should have kept to myself, but they bubbled to the surface regardless of my effort to tamp them down. "I slept with Brett," I blurted.

He groaned and collapsed next to me on the bed. "I'm aware. I was there, but I don't remember much sleeping."

"Is it weird for you? Cuz it's weird for me." Suddenly feeling exposed, I pulled the edge of the comforter over my breasts.

"It's a little weird. I mean... I've never been in this situation before," he said with a sigh.

"Me neither. It's not like I'm a prude, but I've been selective. What happened... it's had me off balance. I thought no one would ever know. I mean, obviously, we've both been with other people before, but seeing..."

"Changed it from theoretical, and what happened between the three of us was very real?"

I nodded. "Are you going to be thinking about him touching me? Are you going to be remembering the things I did? The things he did? The things you both did to me?"

Trent threw his arm over his eyes. "I was trying not to, but you're making it really hard and not in a good way. Can I tell you a secret?"

My ears perked up. Insight into the inner workings of Trent Dorsey's mind piqued my curiosity. "Of course."

He rolled on his side and stared into my eyes. "In all the times Brett and I have pulled that routine, being with you was the first time I've ever felt jealous. It's always been just sex. A means to an end. Everyone walks away happy and satisfied. But that night... I didn't want to share you."

"Then why did you?"

"I thought the feeling was temporary. That once we got upstairs, it would go away. But the moment he kissed you I knew I should have kept you for myself. If I regret anything, it's not telling Brett to fuck off that night, but the plan was already in motion, and I knew I couldn't keep you anyway."

"Yet, here we are."

"Here we are."

"I have one more question. How did the two of you start seducing women together?" The question had been nagging at me since I'd come down from the high of that night.

He chuckled. "Oddly enough, it was a woman. This girl in college taught us how to pleasure a woman. It was awkward at first, but once we became comfortable with our sexuality, it was addicting. Vegas was the perfect place to keep the game going with no strings attached and no one catching feelings."

"Until you met me, and I messed everything up." It sucked knowing I was one in a long line of many women who'd come before me, but I asked, and I had to accept his truth.

Trent pulled the tie that secured my braid and let my hair free. "You didn't mess anything up. You reminded me there was more to life than meaningless one-night stands. You make me feel things I haven't felt in a really long time. So, although tonight isn't our first time together, it feels like the first time for me."

"Me too," I confessed.

"So, let's put the past in the past and start over, just you and me. I don't want you thinking about anyone else tonight." He smoothed out the lines between my eyes with his thumb and pressed a gentle kiss to my forehead.

"I'm only thinking about you. I... I needed to know."

"You're not a conquest. I can't promise you where this is going, but I can promise you I want to find out." He pulled the comforter away from my breasts and ran his fingertips over my nipples.

I rolled onto my back, closed my eyes, and relaxed into his touch, waiting for him to take the next step. When he didn't, I cracked one eye to find him staring down at me.

"Any more questions?" The sincerity in his dark eyes let me know he was waiting for me to give the green light.

"One." I paused. "You gonna fuck me or not?"

"Abso-fucking-lutely. No more waiting. I've waited long enough." Leaning forward, he captured my lips with less gentleness than before. Like a caged tiger that'd finally been set free to devour me, Trent crawled over the top of me and settled between my legs which instinctually wrapped around his waist. Our bare skin pressed together, chest to chest, his hard edges against my soft curves. I felt safe and warm under his dominating presence.

The kiss turned erratic, and my desire grew. Wetness flooded my panties. Remembering the way he felt inside me, I was anxious to get to the main event, but there was no way I'd forgo the foreplay and the orgasms I knew he could deliver.

Trent kissed along my jaw and down my neck and between my breasts. "Have I told you how amazing your tits are?"

I giggled. "Not specifically, but I gathered as much." He sucked one in his mouth and massaged the other in his hand. Taking turns, he made sure each was properly worshipped. With a final nip of his teeth, he pulled one nipple into a taut point and grinned, clearly proud of the moans he'd extracted from me. I grabbed the sides of his head and pressed his face toward my stomach. "Need you lower."

"Getting there." Trent licked a line from my sternum down to my belly button, lashing his tongue in and out like he was sucking vodka from the divot. "Even your stomach is sexy. Flat and toned." He hooked his fingers in the waistband of my shorts and lifted a brow.

I gave him a small nod and lifted my hips. In one fell swoop, he stripped my shorts and panties down my legs and tossed them to the side. Trent stood at the bottom of the bed, hands on his waist and gazed down at me as if I were a feast to be consumed. I'd shaved and applied lotion to every bit of my skin before he arrived, just in case our night turned in this direction, so I was very aware of what he was seeing. Regardless, his intensity made me self-conscious. Feeling bashful, I covered my most private parts with my hands.

"Don't you dare." He grabbed my wrists and pinned them at my sides. "I've been waiting weeks for this. You are nothing but beautiful. Don't hide from me."

I gulped. "You were staring."

"As any man in my position would. You can't blame me for being human." He twined our fingers together and used his knee to push my legs apart, all the while keeping his eyes on mine. The cool air between my thighs made me feel even more exposed. He brought his other knee to the mattress and spread me wider. He kissed me, his tongue swiping inside my mouth. I returned the kiss and let our tongues tangle together, dizzy not only from the kiss but the smell of his cologne, which I'd come to associate with my sexy boss. "Let me show you how beautiful you are."

Trent trailed his lips down the length of my body, until he reached the apex of my thighs. Releasing my hands, he pushed my legs even farther apart and blew a stream of cool air directly on my pussy, sending shivers down my spine.

And then he feasted.

The first swipe of his tongue sent me reeling as he drew figure eights with the tip, delving deeper inside me with every lap until his face was buried completely in my wet heat, which only made me wetter. The small gush that should have embarrassed me only seemed to spur him on.

Trent slipped a finger inside me. "Jesus, baby, you're so tight." He inserted a second finger and used a come-hither motion to stimulate my G-spot, then attacked my clit in all-out warfare.

Licking, nipping, sucking... I couldn't keep track of all he was doing. All I could do was succumb to the sensations zipping through my body. The pressure built and my walls clenched around his fingers, every second bringing me closer to the edge. "Oh fuck, Trent! That feels so good... ahhh!" I gripped the comforter in desperation, my head thrashing back and forth and obscenities pouring from my lips, as I rode the thin line between pleasure and pain. When I was sure I couldn't take anymore, the wave crested and broke, throwing me into an ocean of bliss. Trent continued his assault as wave after wave crashed into me, leaving me helpless and wrung out on the shore.

As my orgasm ebbed, he gifted me one last long swipe of his tongue before pulling a string of condoms from his back pocket and tossing them on the bed. Not one. Not two. At least four condoms lay next to me along with some packets of lube. "Holy shit! For one night?"

Trent pulled his belt through the loops and dropped it to the floor before undoing the button and zipper of his jeans. "I wanted to be prepared."

My eyes widened. "For what? Are you trying to kill me?"

He smirked. "Only in the very best way. Succumbing to multiple orgasms seems like a good way to go." His jeans and boxers were shoved to the floor, leaving him gloriously naked. He stroked his impressive cock slowly, giving it one last tug before reaching for the condoms. "Are you ready for me?"

I bit my lip in anticipation and nodded as the sound of the package ripping filled the room.

Trent rolled the condom down his long length and crawled on the bed between my spread legs. "There're so many things I want to do to you, but right now I need to be inside you."

I wrapped my hand around his cock and caressed him from root to tip, getting my first feel of him in weeks. A hiss escaped his lips as his eyes closed in ecstasy. I lifted my hips and brought him to my entrance. He braced himself over me and slowly pushed inside, my body stretching to accommodate his wide girth. "So good," I murmured.

"So damn good," he whispered back. Trent moved his hips at a leisurely pace, drawing out every stroke, every inch of him massaging me from the inside out. It was pure pleasurable torture, and I loved every second of it.

My arms wrapped around his neck, and I fused our mouths together in a passionate kiss. I wanted to be closer to this man who'd driven me crazy with endless power plays in the office. I might have fought him in the boardroom, but in the bedroom, I'd submit to whatever he wanted. I already knew he'd take good care of me, and I was more than happy to be at his mercy.

Trent lifted my leg and hiked it to his waist, changing the angle and pushing in deeper. "I can't go slow much longer."

"Then don't. Fuck me, Mr. Dorsey."

He growled from deep in his chest, picking up the pace, pistoning into me like a man on a mission. With each stroke his pelvis rubbed against my clit, pushing me closer to orgasm. I was ready to come again, and my walls began to clench. "Don't you dare," he ordered, pulling out and flipping me over. With an arm around my waist, he hoisted me to my knees and impaled me from behind.

My body shook and I fell to my elbows, pressing my cheek to the bed. I snaked one hand between my legs, desperate to get the orgasm he stole from me. He slapped it out of the way. Not capable of much more, I whimpered my complaint and wiggled my ass.

Trent gave it a swift smack. My skin stung. I'd never been spanked before, but I found it erotically arousing. "Don't try to top from the bottom," he scolded. "Your orgasms belong to me. I won't let you take them." He smacked my ass again. My core flooded from the sensation and his commanding tone. "You like that, don't you, Miss Romano?"

I whimpered.

"Answer me." Trent continued to pound into me.

"Yes," I squeaked out.

"I can't hear you."

"Yes," I shouted.

"Good girl. I'll give you what you want." He reached between my legs and rubbed my clit furiously. "Is this what you want?"

"Yes," I shouted again.

With his fingers working my clit and his cock deep in my pussy, the sensations were almost too much. My climax built quickly, my body clenching around him. "Not yet," he growled.

Like I had any control. "I can't…." Trying to hold it back only made it more intense. I was riding the edge, ready to tip over. A series of incoherent expletives fell from my mouth.

"Now!" He doubled down his efforts and I exploded. My eyes rolled back, and my head swam from the inundation of endorphins. I felt like I was flying, soaring through space and time to some unknown destination. I was high as a kite, and I didn't want to come down.

Soft kisses started on my shoulder and trailed down my spine as my body gently floated back to earth. "How do you feel?"

"Like a jellyfish. I'm pretty sure I couldn't move if I wanted to."

He chuckled and tapped my ass that was still up in the air. "Stay put." Pulling out, he walked his naked self to the bathroom.

"No worries." I gave him a thumbs-up from my awkward position on the bed while appreciating his retreating form. My legs slid out from under

152

me, and I collapsed in a heap of boneless flesh. *Wow!* The entire experience was existential. I thought the pleasure I received during our threesome was a unicorn, but tonight proved it existed outside of that little bubble. Sex with my ex was satisfying, but it was never... this. All my life I'd been waiting for a man to take control in the bedroom. Never did I think it would be my boss.

Trent returned with a towel and gently wiped it between my legs, an intimate gesture I wasn't accustomed to. "That was amazing," he said with a kiss to my cheek.

I cracked an eye open. "Meh. It was alright."

"Alright?" He laughed. "Is that why you called out my name over and over?"

"I didn't call out your name." *Did I?* Everything was a blur.

"I assure you, you did. *Trent! Fuck, Trent! Fuck me harder!* You have a filthy mouth, Miss Romano. Some of the words that came out of those pretty little lips would make a sailor blush."

I groaned. "I don't remember any of that. I must have blacked out."

"I'll let you rest before round two."

Round two? I'd barely survived round one.

Trent pulled back the comforter and moved me onto the sheets. Lying behind me, he covered us both and pulled me against his chest. It was warm and cozy, and I felt something I hadn't felt in years... completely content.

153

Chapter 24
Trent

Gia's red hair cascaded over the white sheets. I pushed her limits last night and she'd risen to the occasion spectacularly. It was everything I imagined it would be and more. Flashes of the night raced through my mind. Her plump lips wrapped around my cock. Her tits bouncing as she rode me. Her hips moving in tandem with mine.

I was getting hard just thinking about it, but as spectacular as it was, the most amazing part was waking up next to her. I couldn't remember the last time I spent the entire night with a woman.

My muscles ached as I rolled out of bed and pulled on my boxers. I needed coffee. And food. The ice cream we ate in the middle of the night wasn't cutting it. I stumbled to the kitchen and put a pod into the tiny hotel coffee maker. As it brewed, I opened her fridge in search of food. Besides what I brought last night, there was a take-out container with half a burger in it and a bottle of ketchup, on to plan B. My stomach grumbled as I ordered us room service, requesting all her favorites from yesterday.

It was hard to believe twenty-four hours ago I begged her to give me another chance and today I woke up in her bed. The woman had me vexed

I was starting to seriously question my own sanity because I'd never put this much effort into getting a woman to spend time with me, yet I was fully invested and would do whatever it took.

The coffee maker sputtered to an end, and I added two sugar packets from the caddy using a plastic stirrer to mix it.

"Did you make that for me?" Gia shuffled in with squinty eyes, trying to tame her hair that stuck out in odd directions. She was fucking cute first thing in the morning, wrapped in a silky black robe that hit her midthigh.

"Good morning, sunshine." I handed her the mug and put another pod in the maker for myself.

She took a sip and scrunched up her face before adding a travel-sized creamer to her mug. "I can't believe you're still here," she said, leaning against the counter.

I lifted a brow. "Would you rather I left in the middle of the night?"

She shook her head. "Absolutely not. Last night was incredible, however I thought maybe I was your forbidden fruit and now that you've had me, you'd disappear."

"There are two things wrong with that statement." Frowning, I held up a fist and lifted a finger. "First, it wasn't the first time I've had you." Another finger. "Second, how in the hell could I ghost you? We work in the same office."

Her lips quirked up on one side. "True. So we're doing this?"

"We are. I can't stop thinking about you." I wrapped my arms around her waist and pulled her in for a kiss.

Gia giggled, placing her mug on the counter. "Careful, Mr. Dorsey, you're starting to sound like a stage-five clinger."

I rolled my eyes at her throwing my own words back at me.

She leaned away from my embrace. "But in all seriousness, I can't be careless. There's too much on the line. Whatever happens between us can't affect my job."

"It won't. If you've ever trusted anyone, trust me." The words spewed from my lips without any thought or care. I spoke from the heart, knowing we both had everything to lose.

"I might be crazy, but I believe you."

155

Her words were a balm to my soul. There wasn't a single thing she could ask that I wouldn't do for her. Because what I felt wasn't lust… it was more.

More, as in I had an instinctive need to protect her.

More, as in I wanted her beyond today or tomorrow.

More, as in I could finally see my future.

It was a need so bone deep I'd fall to my knees if necessary. No questions asked. I'd cocoon her in my arms and never let go.

Bewitched.

She put a spell on me and there wasn't a damn thing I could do about it.

"I…" *Love?* It was way too soon to go down that road. "I care about you." They weren't the right words, but they were the best I could do. Veering away from the topic, I looked in her empty fridge. "You have nothing to eat so I ordered room service. You need to go grocery shopping."

"Well, my boss is a tyrant, and I haven't had time to scout out the local grocery stores, nor do I have a car here."

I scowled. "Your boss isn't that bad."

"Yeah, he's beginning to grow on me. Kinda cute too."

A knock on the door signaled the arrival of our breakfast. "Stay put." No way did I want anyone seeing her in that silky robe besides me. I quickly retrieved my jeans and tugged them on before opening the door and giving the nameless service host a generous tip. Just because I didn't know him, didn't mean he didn't recognize me. Discretion was of utmost importance at Mystique and staff were paid well to keep it that way no matter what they saw, however a little more incentive couldn't hurt.

I wheeled the cart inside and unloaded it on the table. "Your breakfast, madam."

Gia took a seat and scooped scrambled eggs onto her plate. "You're spoiling me. I feel like all we've done since Friday is eat."

"We can work it off later." I waggled my brows and sat across from her. "Now, about your car. I assume you had one if you were driving from Waukegan to Chicago every day."

She swallowed. "I did, but I wasn't sure what the situation would be here, so I sold it to my sister. I shipped my stuff to the hotel and hopped on a plane with my suitcases. I figured I could use Lyft or Uber or even a taxi until I got my bearings."

The thought of her in a car with some stranger didn't sit well with me. "Those are options, but I can take you somewhere if needed. We're going to be spending a lot of time together anyway."

"Is that so? You'll be my own personal chauffeur?"

"I will. After breakfast, I'll take you grocery shopping and we can stop anywhere else you need." Domesticity had never been my thing, but suddenly buying eggs and orange juice with her appealed to me.

Definitely bewitched.

Chapter 25
Gia

"Good Morning, Miss Romano," Trent said as he poked his head into my office.

"Good morning, Mr. Dorsey."

"I'll need you in my office in ten minutes. Don't be late."

I lifted a manicured brow. "I rarely am."

He tapped on his watch and disappeared down the hallway.

"Okay, I'm going to ask," Penny said, throwing her hands in the air. "What the hell is going on with you two? You've been acting weird for weeks."

Trent and I were extra careful not to let our romance spill over into the office since we made it official. "Weird how?"

She squinted her eyes at me. "Don't be coy with me, missy. I remember you threatening to poke his eyes out with a pen when you first started here. Now it's all... *Good morning, Mr. Dorsey. Right away, Mr. Dorsey. Of course, Mr. Dorsey*," she mimicked.

I signed my name on the document in front of me in an effort to seem unaffected. "We've come to an agreement to be cordial for the purposes of work. It makes it much easier than when I want to strangle him."

"Uh-huh. Just as I suspected." She leaned back in her chair and crossed her arms.

I threw my pen down. "What is?"

"You two have the hots for each other, don't you?"

I let out a sigh of exasperation. Trent and I spent almost every night together over the past few weeks. Keeping this secret from Penny felt shitty, but it was entirely necessary. "You're being ridiculous. We've been nothing but professional."

"Too professional," she mused. "You used to come in here and vent about him being an asshole, but for the last month… nothing. You haven't complained one bit about him being demanding or making unreasonable requests. Absolutely nothing. It's as fishy as the Shark Reef at Mandalay Bay."

"I've never been there, so I wouldn't know." I tapped the side of my head. "Think about it, Penny, you're dating his best friend. Don't you think he would have told Brett if we were involved?"

Her lips scrunched to one side. "Maybe, but I still think you're hiding something."

"Perhaps it's your own guilt," I said, trying to redirect her attention. "You've barely told me anything about you and Brett. You're the one who's hiding something and so you assume I am too."

She sagged. "What do you want to know?"

I folded my hands under my chin and leaned on my desk. "Only everything." I listened for the next ten minutes as Penny spilled the details of her blossoming relationship. I'll admit I got more than I bargained for. Seemed Brett wasn't the only one into kinky shit. My little wallflower of an assistant had her own proclivities. By the time she finished talking, Trent and I were the last thing on her mind.

My ears might have been bleeding, but my objective was accomplished.

159

I shut the door behind me and flipped the lock.

"You're late, Miss Romano." Trent beckoned me with his finger, making my panties wet with the simple action.

I strode to his desk in my three-inch heels, giving my hips a little extra sway. "I assure you, Mr. Dorsey, I have a good excuse." I liked this game we played at work. Sitting on the edge of his desk in front of him, I left my legs a few inches apart, knowing he wouldn't be able to resist the temptation.

Hidden behind his desk, he ran his hands up my legs and inside the edge of my panties, slipping a single finger into my pussy. The forbidden touch made me forget everything but the feel of him stroking inside me. "Hmmm. What could be so important that you've kept me waiting?"

"We have a problem," I muttered as he inserted a second finger.

"The only problem is you should be bent over my desk right now, with my cock inside you instead of my fingers." He pumped in and out of me, pressing his thumb against my clit in a circular motion.

I loved indulging in the naughty office behavior we should have kept at bay. My body tingled and fluttered under his expert ministrations. "I...I...." I couldn't for the life of me remember a single thing I was supposed to say.

"You what?" Trent increased the tempo and pressure until an orgasm seized me and I fell over the edge, breath caught in my throat and body humming. "So damn beautiful," he groaned.

With his fingers still inside me and the fog clearing from my head, I spit out a single word. "Brett."

He frowned. "Not exactly the name I want to hear when I've just made you come."

I grabbed his arm as he went to pull his hand from under my skirt. "And Penny. They're onto us," I explained. "We need to tell them before they figure it out on their own."

Trent ran his hand down my leg in a gentle caress. "Brett's not a problem. I trust him completely. The question is, do you trust Penny?"

I nodded. "She hasn't given me any reason not to, and honestly, I feel like a bad friend not telling her. If they find out from someone else, they'll both be hurt."

He pulled a wipe from his desk and cleaned his fingers. "Hunter is coming back from Albuquerque at the end of the week. We're going to have to be more careful. If he suspects anything…"

I put a hand on his shoulder. "Which is why this might be the perfect time. It would be nice to have allies in case something goes awry."

"It's up to you," he said with a quick peck to my lips. "If you trust Penny, then so do I."

"I do. When should we tell them?"

"Tonight. Invite Penny for drinks at The Rabbit Hole. Call it a girls' night. I'll bring Brett. We haven't hung out in a while, so he'll be totally up for it. Seven o'clock?"

"We're either going to have allies or two friends who are really pissed at us."

Trent smoothed out the lines between my eyebrows with his thumb. "You worry too much. Everything's going to work out. You'll see."

I wished I had his confidence. If something went wrong, it would cost both of us.

Chapter 26
Trent

"About time. I've barely seen you lately." Brett said, taking a sip of his scotch.

I held my glass up to his. "I'm not the only one to blame. You've been busy too."

Brett's mouth quirked up on one side. "True. Penny has been a pleasant surprise. There's way more to her than meets the eye."

"Funny how I barely knew she existed before Gia started working at Mystique." The truth was Suzette probably bullied her into being a wallflower. Penny had lots of good ideas, but she never got to have a voice.

"Would it be crazy to say she's the most normal woman I've ever dated? She couldn't care less about my money. I took her to a fancy restaurant, and she ordered chicken. It was the cheapest thing on the menu. I expected her to order lobster or a filet mignon. It's refreshing, to say the least."

I chuckled as I sipped my own scotch. "Gia did the same thing when I took her out. She wanted a corn dog." It was too late to take the words back when I realized my gaffe.

Brett lifted a brow. "Something you want to tell me, friend? Have you finally manned up and admitted she's perfect for you?"

I pressed my lips together. Gia and I were supposed to do this together and I let the cat out of the bag. It was impossible to stuff it back in now. I'd already all but admitted we were dating.

Gia and Penny strutted into the bar, saving me from having to say anything. Brett saw where my focus was and snapped his eyes in their direction. "Well, isn't this a coincidence?" he muttered. Before I knew it, he was out of his seat and leading the ladies in our direction. With a peck to Penny's cheek, he pulled out her chair. "Fancy meeting you two here." Gia and I played the *I Hate You* game we'd been practicing for weeks, a few sideward glances and a shit ton of space between us. "I think our friends have something to tell us."

Penny stared at Gia and me. "What am I missing?"

Brett summoned the waitress and ordered drinks for the table. "It's not my story to tell." His voice was laced with a sense of betrayal I'd never heard before.

"Gia?" Penny asked

"We're together," Gia blurted. So much for easing them into the situation.

Penny pulled back. "Who's together?" She pointed between us. "You two?"

The hurt in Penny's voice kick-started my brain. I wrapped my arm around Gia's shoulders. "We didn't plan it. It just... sort of happened."

Penny leaned into Brett. "Did you know about this?"

"Not a clue," he responded.

Penny pinned Gia with a look of disappointment. "So, all this time, I've been pouring my heart out to you, and you lied to me?"

"It wasn't a lie," Gia defended. "I just didn't tell you the whole truth. Please, don't be mad."

"I'm not mad," Penny said. "I'm..."

"Hurt," Brett finished, setting his sights on me. "You've been my best friend since fifth grade, and you didn't think you could tell me? I practically pushed you in Gia's direction. I knew you were perfect for each other."

"You did?" Gia asked.

"From the first time we met," he said.

This was going nowhere good, and fast. They may not like our reasoning, but they'd have to accept it. I held up my hand. "We get it. You feel deceived, but please hear us out." I pointed to my chest. "My job is on the line."

"So is mine," Gia interrupted. "Coming to Vegas was a gamble. No one thought I belonged here. If people find out Trent and I are dating, they'll think I got the job because I'm sleeping with my boss. I want to earn respect, not be the subject of office gossip. I need to prove myself so I'm not a joke."

Penny's face fell. "You're not a joke. I worked for two people before you and you're by far the best event coordinator we've had. No one can touch your work ethic or dedication."

"Director of entertainment and events," I corrected. "And I agree. I may be biased, but Gia has done amazing work."

"I understand Gia's need for secrecy." Penny waved her hand in my direction. "What's your excuse for not telling your best friend?"

"Daddy Dearest threatened to fire him if he didn't keep his dick in his pants," Brett offered. Penny gasped as I glared at him. "My bet is, he thought I'd tell you and that was a problem."

Penny snuggled into Brett's side as she spoke to Gia. "You didn't trust me?"

"I wanted to, but I didn't know you that well. I was afraid it would change things."

I wrapped a protective arm around Gia's shoulders. "We both have a lot to lose. You can judge us if you want, but we'd prefer you don't."

"Is this why Hunter is in Albuquerque?" Brett asked.

I gave him a stiff nod. "He's been sniffing around like a rabid dog. He'd like nothing more than to take my job and I'm not giving him the firepower to do it. However, he'll be back at the end of the week. If he even gets an inkling something is going on between us, he won't hesitate to rat me out. If Gia and I decide this is going to be a long-term relationship, I'll tell my father on my own terms. So, even if it feels like we betrayed you, we did what we felt we had to do. It wasn't a fuck you. I promise."

164

Brett stared at me long and hard, his jaw clenched tight. I gave it right back. He knew what was on the line. He knew I couldn't risk it. Finally, he picked up his drink and took a sip. "I, for one, am thrilled at this turn of events. It explains why you haven't been such a moody pain in the ass lately."

I sighed with relief. Brett and I promised a woman would never come between us, and I put it to the test with Gia.

She took Penny's hand over the table. "I'm sorry I wasn't honest, but after our discussion today, I couldn't keep it from you any longer. Forgive me."

"I should have figured it out sooner. I can see now all the bickering and heated exchanges were foreplay. I wish you would have confided in me, but I understand why you didn't."

Gia squeezed Penny's hand. "Thank you. I'm so fortunate to have met you and become your friend. I don't take that for granted."

Brett slapped the table. "This calls for a celebration!" He flagged down the waitress and ordered another round, even though our glasses were half-full. He held up what was left of his drink. "To my friend who has finally met his match." He looked down at Penny adoringly. "And the woman who has helped me pull my head out of my ass. I'd say we're both lucky bastards."

We clinked our glasses together. Deep down, I always knew Brett wouldn't turn his back on me. I was glad Penny was as devoted to Gia, and our secret was safe.

"Well, look who's returned."

"Hardy har har," Hunter said as he entered my office.

"You look well. How was Albuquerque?" I steepled my fingers and tapped the tips together as I leaned back in my chair.

"Not Vegas." He walked over to the bookshelf and inspected the pictures, rearranging them as he went. My brother had a bad habit of touching my shit just to get a rise out of me. "What did I miss? Anything new I should know about?"

"Not a thing," I said without missing a beat.

He quirked a brow at me. "You sure about that?"

"Positive. It's been smooth sailing. Everything's running like clockwork."

"And our new event coordinator?"

Of course he would ask about Gia. His dick had been standing at attention ever since she arrived. "She's working out quite well, very organized and professional." I kept it vague, giving him nothing to sink his claws into."

"Hmmm. Dad and Rose coming back next week?"

It pissed me off that he called my mom by her first name. She'd been more of a mother to him than the piece of crap that gave birth to him and dropped him on our doorstep. "Next Thursday... just in time for the fundraiser."

"I guess we'll see what happens then."

His cryptic statement annoyed me. "With what?"

"Everything."

"Knock, knock." Gia breezed into my office, waving a piece of paper in the air, stopping short when she saw Hunter. "Oh, I didn't realize you were here."

He looked her up and down with a smug smirk. "Miss me?"

She pasted on a fake smile. "It's good to have you back." Turning to me, she held up the paper and slid it across my desk.

"What's this?"

She nodded to the document. "Read it. I think you'll be pleased, Mr Dorsey." She knew what she was doing. My cock twitched at the formality A tease and a temptress.

I skimmed the paper, more than thrilled at what I read. "You got her?"

166

Gia barely contained her excitement. "It's only for two weeks, as a trial period, with an agreement to renegotiate. Scarlet knew somebody who knew somebody…" She waved her hand around. "Anyway, it got me an in."

"This is good news. Excellent work, Miss Romano. I'll see that you're rewarded accordingly." I was already imagining the ways I'd reward her. I'd order a bottle of champagne and drink it out of her pussy, then fuck her 'til neither of us could walk in the morning.

"Anyone care to share the"—Hunter finger quoted—"good news."

I set the signed contract on my desk. "It seems Miss Romano has secured a residency with Ariel Fox. This is going to make us more competitive as an entertainment venue."

Hunter started a slow clap. "Well, haven't you been a busy little beaver. We should go out and celebrate."

There was no way in hell that was happening. He'd have to crawl over my dead body to get anywhere near her beaver.

"That's a nice offer," Gia said. "But like you said, busy, busy, busy. With the fundraiser right around the corner, there's too much to do."

"Surely, you have an hour to spend with your boss. Trent can't be working you that hard, or is he?" Hunter quipped with a lift of his brow.

Gia looked at him like a deer in headlights.

I thought the time away would have given him some perspective, but clearly, I was mistaken. That was two inappropriate comments within a minute. "First of all, you're not her boss. I am. Secondly, she said no. I won't have you making her feel guilty for doing her job."

"Her job? Is that what we're calling it?" He tapped a finger against his lips. "Of course, you're referring to the fundraiser." He winked at Gia. "Congratulations. Some other time perhaps. I think you would find working under me has its own benefits. Maybe one day we can make that happen."

I slammed my fist on the desk. "That's enough!"

"I'm quite happy where I am," she interrupted, holding out a hand for me to stop. My instinct was to protect her from my slimeball brother. If he said another inappropriate thing, so help me God, I'd do a fuckton more than break his nose. "Trent has treated me nothing but professionally and for you to suggest otherwise is completely insulting. Don't think I've missed your not-so-subtle innuendos or the way you look at me like a steak dinner. I was patient before, but my patience has run out. If you continue to sexually harass me, I'll have no choice but to report you. I hope I am being clear when I say I have no interest in getting a drink with you or any other extracurricular activities you've imagined."

Hunter stuck his hands in his pockets as if the words she'd said meant nothing to him. "Is that a threat, Ms. Romano?"

"It's a promise. I deserve more than to be treated like a piece of meat."

I was proud of Gia for speaking up. It was that fire that drew me to her in the first place.

"I see I've been barking up the wrong tree. If it's professional you want, then I'll follow the corporate handbook to the *T*. You've made yourself quite clear. Crystal, in fact." Hunter tugged on the lapels of his suit coat.

"Thank you. I appreciate your understanding."

"I'm a reasonable man, Gia. You'd know that if you had given me a chance."

"It's not personal," she defended.

"That's where you're wrong. In this business, everything is personal." He gave me a curt nod and headed out of my office. "I'll leave you two to your *business*."

When the door clicked behind him, Gia let out a quiet, "Fuck." She fell into the chair opposite my desk. "I totally fucked that up. I should have let it go."

"You didn't fuck it up. If I'd kept defending you, it would have looked suspicious. He needed to hear it from you. You've set the boundaries. If he steps over them, it's on him.

"I suppose."

"You know what else?" I asked, leaning over my desk.

She let out a huff. "What?"

"That was sexy as hell. I got a stiffy watching you put him in his place."

She laughed. "You're ridiculous."

"Come home with me tonight." The words left my lips before I could pull them back. It was the first time I'd invited a woman to my apartment since Morgan. Trust wasn't something I handed out freely, but with Gia, all my walls were down. It was time to take the next step.

"You're serious?"

"Completely. I want to see all that gorgeous red hair spread across my black sheets."

"Careful, Mr. Dorsey," she said with a smile. "You're getting a little clingy. If I didn't know better, I'd venture to say you might be falling."

"Sweetheart, I fell for you the first time you called me an asshole." And it scared the shit out of me. I should have been running but all I could seem to do was pull her closer. I'd never been this happy. She chased away all the darkness I harbored and let light shine into my life.

I asked her to trust me, but what I didn't know was that I would be the one to trust her. *Implicitly.*

Chapter 27
Gia

Trent's apartment was like nothing I'd ever seen before. I dropped my overnight bag by the door and walked toward the panel of windows that took up one whole wall. The city glittered like diamonds in the dark.

Trent handed me a glass of wine. "It's beautiful, isn't it?"

"Yes. There are days this all seems like a dream. I'm doing what everyone said I couldn't."

"Good thing you didn't listen to them." He opened the slider and led me out to the balcony.

I grabbed onto the railing with one hand and lifted the glass to my lips with the other. A gentle breeze tossed my hair around my shoulders. It was quieter here. On the Strip there was always a hum of noise and activity. Horns honking. People talking and laughing. A bang here, a boom there. But on this balcony, removed from the heart of the city, it was peaceful. "Thank you for sharing this with me."

His hand ran down my spine and rested on the small of my back. "There's no one I'd rather share it with." He pressed his lips to mine in a gentle kiss that heated quickly.

I hung my arms over his shoulders, letting the glass dangle from my fingertips as we devoured each other. He moved us to the lounger, and I straddled his lap, my skirt riding up my thighs. I emptied my glass and set it on the side table. "What do you think you're doing, Mr. Dorsey?"

He pulled the blouse from my skirt, his fingers dancing along my bare skin. "Loving on you."

I placed my hands over his. "Someone could see us."

He shook his head. "It's totally private. It's too dark and we're too high up for anyone to see. I don't want anyone getting a peek at what's mine."

Mine.

That one word sent my heart fluttering. All my life I'd followed the rules, doing the right thing. I colored inside the lines.

Until I met Trent with his persuasive and talented tongue. Since then, I'd been crossing lines right and left with a big red crayon.

And I liked it.

I glanced to the sides, saw the walls that shielded us from the neighbors and lifted my blouse over my head. It was naughty and freeing.

Trent reached behind my back and unclasped my bra, pulling the straps down my shoulders. "Gorgeous." He played with my breasts, kneading them and sucking my nipples. I rocked against the bulge in his pants, shamelessly grinding my clit along his erection. "Take my cock out."

This bossy side of him turned me on. I scooted back and quickly went to work on his belt and zipper. His cock sprang free, all thick and veiny. My fingers wrapped around him, and I used my thumb to spread the precum all over the engorged head.

Trent groaned and pushed my skirt up around my hips. He slipped my panties to the side and finger fucked me. "You're so goddamn wet for me."

I was. He wound me up so tight I was ready to go off like a firework. He always made sure I came before him. I'd been selfish, taking without giving. Tonight, I felt generous.

I pushed my hips back until his fingers fell from inside me. "Hey…"

My finger went to his lips. "Shhh. Let me take care of you." I shimmied backward until my body lay flat on his legs and took him in my mouth. My tongue licked from his balls to the head, savoring the salty taste. Taking him to the back of my throat, I swallowed and took him deeper.

His hips bucked. "Jesus Christ, Gia!" His hands gripped the sides of my head and guided me up and down at a languid pace. I tilted my head, so each stroke rubbed his cock along the rigid roof of my mouth and down to the tight cavern of my throat. He was a lot to take, but I enjoyed the challenge. His steady stream of filthy words assured me my technique was on point.

Trent gripped me under the arms and pulled me back on his lap. "When I come, I want it to be inside you." With some awkward adjustments, he managed to push his pants down his hips and pull a condom from his wallet. Ripping my panties, he tossed them to the floor. I frowned at the tattered lace. "They were in the way."

"You owe me."

"Happily. Now get on me."

With my hands on his shoulders, I sank down, easing his cock into my pussy. He was bigger than any other man I'd been with and filled me full, stretching my body in the most delicious way. "Fuck, yes. Feels so good," I moaned.

I rocked my hips forward and back, rubbing myself against his pelvis. Trent sucked my tits while one hand ran down the crack of my ass. He pushed his thumb inside and I clenched.

"Easy, baby. Let me in," he cooed in my ear.

I fought the impulse to keep him out and relaxed into the feel of his forbidden touch. My body came alive. Every nerve ending sparked to life. My brain swam with endorphins. I climbed higher and higher, ready to explode. "I'm gonna come." My head fell back as the orgasm overtook me and my body quivered with the release.

Trent pumped harder and faster, gripping my hips so hard I was sure to have bruises in the morning. With one final thrust, his eyebrows narrowed and his mouth fell open. "Fuck, baby! Yes!"

With my skirt still pushed up around my waist, I collapsed onto his chest, fully satisfied. Trent tenderly ran his fingers through my hair, cradling my head. Neither of us said a word as we basked in the afterglow of amazing sex.

I had teased him about falling for me, but the truth was I'd fallen in love with him. It happened too fast. Too messy. The roller-coaster ride of emotions overwhelmed me.

And it scared the crap out of me because I wasn't sure Trent was capable of love.

Trent dropped me off at Mystique early to avoid prying eyes. I felt safe behind the tinted windows of his Audi but getting out cast me into the light. I bowed my head and made my way to the elevators, avoiding eye contact with anyone.

"Late night?"

The French accent was unmistakable. Genevieve fiddled with the floral arrangement in the lobby. "I…um…I…"

She held up a hand. "No explanation required. You're glowing, *mon chéri*. A healthy sexual appetite is good for the soul. I hope he's deserving of you."

I pushed my hair behind my ears. "I'm not sure yet, but I'm hoping he is. Can you pretend you didn't see me sneaking in?"

She zipped her lips. "A lady is entitled to secrets. Some of the best moments are those we can't tell anyone about."

"Is that so?" I said coyly, glad my indiscretions were safe with Genevieve. "Are you speaking from experience?"

She shrugged. "I've had a lover or two. I may be old, but I'm not dead."

I laughed. "Thank you." Giving her a tight hug, I continued my walk of shame, but I didn't feel shameful at all. I deserved the good *D* I was getting.

A shower and a coffee later, I walked into the office on cloud nine. Whether my relationship with Trent lasted or not, I hadn't ever felt so desired.

"Tone it down, will you?" Penny said.

"I can't help it. The sex is amazing." I smacked a hand over my lips. "Pretend I didn't say that."

Penny hugged me tightly. "No take backs. I'm so happy for you, even if I'm confused how you could fall for Trent. He's so…"

"Bossy," I finished.

"Yes. Although that's not exactly the word I was thinking. He's an…"

"Asshole?"

"I didn't say that, but if the suit fits.

"I get it. I really do, but there's a side to him you don't know."

"You can't help who you fall in love with."

"Who said anything about love?" It was presumptuous for Penny to assume anything.

"Sheesh, girl. I may not have been privy to all the dirty details, but I'm not blind. You're totally in love with your boss."

I held a finger to my lips. "Shhhh. Nobody needs to know. I've barely admitted it to myself, let alone told him."

"You've got it bad. If you don't want anyone to know, you better wipe that shit-eating grin off your face."

I ran a hand over my face, trying to make it disappear. "Better?"

"Marginally." She dropped into a chair. "What's on the plan for the day?"

"Ariel Fox. I want to make sure we have everything on her rider correct. This is big. If we get it right, it could be worth beaucoup bucks for Mystique. My new title depends on it."

"I seriously doubt that," she said, pulling a pen from her mass of curls.

"Maybe not, but consider it insurance if anything goes wrong. I want her residency locked down. If I get fired, it won't be for incompetency." No matter how careful we'd been, I wasn't oblivious to the risk I was taking.

"You're not getting fired."

I wished I had her confidence. Trent was my ace in the hole, but Hunter was a wild card. Our interaction the day before unsettled me. The guy was out for blood and at this point I don't think he cared whose he got. "Insurance isn't a bad thing."

Penny made some notes on her pad of paper. "Consider it done." Sticking the pen back in her hair, she said, "And for the record, I haven't been Trent's biggest fan. That being said, he's been way more tolerable of late. If that has anything to do with you, then I'm all for this love affair."

"I feel like I'm in a dream." I pulled my hair up in a loose ponytail, wrapped it around my hand, and let it fall back to my shoulders. "I'm living in Vegas, have a career I love, and a man who accepts me for who I am. It's too perfect. I keep waiting for something to go wrong. There's no way this can last."

Penny shook her head at me. "Don't self-sabotage. You should soak it all up. Things are going well because you worked damn hard to get here. What are you worried about.?"

The list of worries was endless, but they all boiled down to one. "Failure. No matter how good it feels, I can't help thinking that being with Trent is a dumb move. I hate sneaking around. It's like walking on eggshells, always looking over my shoulder. Why did I have to fall for the one guy that's off-limits?"

"Uh... because he makes all your lady parts tingle."

"True. But at what cost? I mean... what if this whole arrangement is temporary? What happens to my job?"

Penny frowned. "You're borrowing trouble. Live for today. You have no control over tomorrow or the day after that."

"You're right." I pasted on a smile I didn't really feel. Regardless of everything Penny said, there was an insecurity that niggled at the back of my brain. I couldn't help but feel like our relationship was a train speeding down a one-way track at two hundred miles per hour with no idea what lies ahead.

If I didn't want to crash and burn, I needed to slow down.

Chapter 28
Trent

I'd barely seen Gia all day. She'd been holed up in her office since the morning. I sent her a text. **Your presence is needed in my office immediately... No panties**. I chuckled. She liked me bossy in bed, but at work... not so much.

I stared at my phone, waiting for a response. When none came, I fired off another. **Miss Romano... you're keeping me waiting.**

I woke her up with my head between her thighs and my tongue in her pussy. She seemed fine when I dropped her off at the hotel. More than fine. I thought we were good, but now I wasn't so sure.

Her popping into my office at random times during the day became the norm and now that she hadn't... I fucking missed her. It was strange. I didn't get tied up in women. Since when did I care if a woman ghosted me? It was preferred, actually. Clingy was a trait I hated. I should have been elated she wasn't hanging out in my office eight hours a day. So, why did I feel like something was missing?

When she didn't respond to my second text, I buzzed Tom. Within seconds, he stood in front of me, notebook at the ready. It was almost comical. "Sir?"

Even though I'd corrected him a million times, I let his faux pas go. "I need you to fetch Miss Romano for me."

He nodded. "I'm on it."

I spun my pen around my fingers as I waited. She may have ignored a text, but she'd never ignore my summons, even if it pissed her off. Which I was counting on. I loved when she got all fiery... lips puckered, cheeks aglow, and eyes narrowed into thin slits. She was a hot-tempered beauty. It was sexy as fuck.

The longer she kept me waiting, the harder my dick got. I tapped my pen against the mahogany desk to the rhythm in my head.

The door flew open, but instead of Gia, Tom stood there huffing as if he'd run the entire way. He pushed his glasses up. "She said she's busy."

"Busy?" *What the fuck.* "Busy doing what?"

"She didn't say. Just that she'd get back with you later."

Later? "I see. Thank you, Tom." He slunk out as if he'd never been there at all.

Something was definitely amiss. If she wouldn't come to me, then I'd go to her. I adjusted my dick and told him to stand down. Even in the beginning, when we fought like cats and dogs, never had she told me *later.*

Strolling down the hall, I loosened my tie, ready to put my woman in her place. I passed Penny's desk and pointed at Gia's door.

"I wouldn't go in there if I were you. She's been in beast mode all day."

Hmmm. "I'll take my chances." I gave a swift knock before letting myself in.

Gia sat on the floor in the middle of the room, shoes kicked off, surrounded by boxes, some open with their contents spilling out. She looked up from the clipboard she was writing on. "Hey."

"Hey? I don't see you all day and all I get is *hey?*"

"Sorry," she said, returning to her clipboard. "I have a lot going on."

"I can see that. What's all this?" I asked, motioning to the boxes.

"These are all the items that came in for the silent auction. Apparently, domestic abuse made everyone feel extra charitable. It's twice what I was expecting. The packages started coming this morning and haven't stopped. I need to open everything, categorize it, and get it ready for Penny to print the description sheets."

It seemed tedious and a waste of her talent. "Why isn't Penny doing this?"

Gia huffed. "First of all, Penny isn't my slave, she's my assistant. Second, I've had her in touch with Ariel Fox's people, making accommodations. She's also calling all our vendors to confirm for the fundraiser. I don't want any surprises. It's a lot to do in a short amount of time."

"I see." I checked my watch. "It's almost five. Are you about ready for dinner?"

"I'll have to pass. I want to get this done tonight, so I'll grab something in the bar with Claude later."

I frowned. Claude was far from a threat, however, it didn't sit right with me.

Penny came in carrying another armload of boxes. "These were just delivered." She set them down among the others.

"Alright. I'll have these sheets ready for you first thing Monday morning. Go enjoy your weekend."

"I can stay," Penny offered. "I'm sure Brett will understand if I need to cancel on him."

Gia waved her away. "Absolutely not. Thank you, but I've got this."

"If you're sure…"

"I'm positive. Go on."

"Okay. I've got a couple little things to do, then I'm outa here." Penny scooted out the door, leaving us alone.

I walked over to Gia's wall with papers tacked all over it. Each one was for a different vendor with handwritten messages and a big pink sticky note with the word *confirmed*. Her methods may have been old-fashioned, but her results were undeniable. "Don't worry. Penny has electronic files of everything. It's all up to company standards," Gia said from her spot on the floor, mistaking my perusal for disapproval.

"I wasn't worried. You're more than organized." I pulled my tie through the collar of my shirt and tossed it on a chair. "What can I do to help?"

Gia blinked up at me. "You don't have to. I'm sure you have other things to do tonight other than going through a bunch of boxes."

In the past, I'd never give up my Friday night for another employee, especially a subordinate. But Gia was so much more than an employee and the only time I wanted her under me was in the bedroom. I undid the top two buttons of my shirt and sat cross-legged on the floor next to her. "Put me to work."

"If you insist." She smiled and handed me a box. "Go on eBay and find a fair market value on this."

I reached into the box and pulled out a football, encased in glass, signed by all the Raiders. "They didn't include a monetary amount?"

"Nope, but there are similar items online. It takes a bit of research, but we need to determine an opening bid."

"Alright." I went to work and researched a dozen different items that came in without the necessary information.

Gia filled out sheet after sheet and placed them on top of the auction items as she lined them up along the walls of her office. This was, by far, going to be the biggest silent auction we'd ever run. By eight o'clock, we only had a few boxes left. She plopped on the floor next to me and stretched her legs out. "What are we doing, Trent?"

I lifted a brow. "Not having sex like I planned."

Her lips quirked up on one side. "Obviously. I mean... what are we doing? Is it just sex?"

My stomach turned. The safe answer would be to not let my heart get involved, but it was too late. "Why do we need to put a label on it?"

She shrugged. "Don't get me wrong, it's been fun but I'm tired of looking over my shoulder all the time. I need some space."

"Space?"

179

"Yes. We've been reckless. With Hunter back and your father returning next week, it's too risky. I'm becoming addicted to the orgasms you give me."

"Addicted?" I laughed because she wasn't the only one, I'd become quite addicted to her myself. It wasn't only the orgasms though. I was addicted to everything about her. The way she smelled. Her smart mouth and the way her soft body felt pressed up against mine.

Gia playfully slapped me on the shoulder. "You know what I mean. The sneaking around is making me sick to my stomach. It's only a matter of time before we get caught."

I took her face in my palm. "It's not just sex. Give us a week. Let's get through the fundraiser and then I'll tell my dad about us. This isn't a hookup. It's so much more than that."

She blinked her blue eyes at me. "Yeah?"

"Yes. I'm not sure exactly where it's going, but I'm not ready to give you up."

Chapter 29
Gia

The week flew by. I dotted every *i* and crossed every *t*. Not a single detail of the Unmask Domestic Abuse fundraiser was left to chance. My days were fast and furious, but my nights were long and luxurious, filled with more attention from a man than I'd ever had in my life.

Penny and I spent Saturday in the salon, getting primped and pampered for an event neither of us thought we'd be attending. My nails and lips were painted a deep burgundy and my eyes a smokey charcoal gray. My hair was curled and pinned back from my face, letting the rest cascade down my back. I ran my hands down the bodice of the emerald, sequined dress and over my hips as I inspected myself in the mirror. Thanks to Trent, it was the most exquisite dress I'd ever worn, and it fit me like a glove. My breasts looked full and my waist tiny. The slit up the side showed enough leg to be borderline scandalous.

There was just one detail left. I lifted the custom mask from the tissue paper and admired the sequins and peacock feathers that adorned it. I tied the satin ribbons around my head and gazed at myself one last time, barely recognizing the woman who stared back at me. I grabbed my clutch and headed for the elevator.

Trent and I decided to arrive separately to maintain the charade. As the elevator hit the lobby and the doors opened, I took a deep breath. I just needed to get through tonight. Next week we'd come clean.

I proceeded to the ballroom, sidled up to the bar, and ordered a martini from Claude. "You look beautiful tonight, Miss Gia."

"Thank you, Claude. How did you know it was me?"

"You can't hide behind that mask. Your hair gives you away," he said with a wink as he made my drink.

I shouldn't have indulged, but one before dinner to settle my nerves wouldn't hurt. In addition to the event running smoothly, I was nervous about my speech. I practiced it on Trent, and he assured me the money would be flowing. I'd spent time at two local women's shelters listening to stories of survivors who were allowing me to share their experiences. It was heartbreaking and real. Domestic abuse was something that happened to "other" people. No one wanted to admit it could happen to someone they knew. There was a level of shame that should have been reserved for the abusers, not the victims.

Placing my glass on the bar top, Claude nodded over my shoulder. "Incoming."

"Well, well, well, aren't you a walking felony."

I didn't have to look to know who it was. "Is that meant as a compliment, Hunter?" I asked, lifting my martini to my lips.

He leaned on the bar and locked eyes with me. "Of course. You look sensational. As a matter of fact, everything does. I can't remember the last time we had a gala this extravagant."

Although he made me leery, the compliment was much appreciated. "Thank you. I apologize for my outburst last week. I hope we can move forward with no hard feelings." Despite his crude behavior, I had no interest in making enemies with him.

"No apology necessary. If anyone should apologize, it's me. I was out of line, but you can't blame a guy for trying. Office romances rarely work anyway so it's probably for the best. Wouldn't you agree?"

I cringed. "Absolutely. There's no sense making things messy." I dreaded having to eat those words when Trent and I went public, but it was a necessary evil at the moment.

"Yes. Nobody likes messy. It can be very unpleasant." Ordering a scotch from the bartender, he tipped his glass at me. "Enjoy your evening, Gia."

Glad to be rid of him for now, I took my glass and ambled over to the tables set up for the silent auction. It was an impressive array of donated items, including sports memorabilia, spa packages, weekend getaways, and a myriad of other bidworthy prizes. Thanks to Penny, the bidding was completely electronic. It was a genius idea. Even at formal events, everyone carried their phone.

"Everything looks amazing!" Penny squealed as she grabbed my arm. "You really pulled this off."

I hugged her tightly. "*We* did. I couldn't have done any of this without you." She looked beautiful in a black satin gown and matching mask with black feathers.

"You both worked hard and should be proud of yourselves," Brett chimed in from behind Penny. He looked handsome in his tux. I'd never forget the night of our threesome, but I didn't feel an ounce of attraction toward him.

My heart was locked on another man. Maybe if Brett had been the one to approach me first or challenge me day in and day out, I'd feel differently, but all I felt was happiness for my quirky assistant and new best friend. Brett was a good guy and Penny deserved a man who would treat her right. "Thank you, Brett." I looked over his shoulder, but Trent was nowhere in sight.

"He's mingling with the board members. You're seated at our table, so you'll see him at dinner," Brett said. "I know this is hard, but Trent is loyal. He'll make things right."

I sighed. "I wish it were already out in the open so we could enjoy the night together."

Leaving Penny and Brett, I wandered around the ballroom, making sure everything was as planned. The jazz band played a sultry tune while the photographer snapped pictures of couples dressed to the nines against the

New Orleans background. Everyone was having a great time, laughing and drinking. Even the fortune-teller, which Trent was adamantly against, had a line of willing participants. I wasn't sure if I believed in the hocus-pocus, but it was fun, nonetheless.

I mingled with the guests and double-checked with our employees, making sure there were no issues that needed my attention. To my delight, it was all running smoothly.

A tap on my shoulder drew my attention. "Everything is perfect, including you, Miss Romano."

"Why thank you, Mr. Dorsey." Trent looked delectable in his tuxedo, custom fit for his broad shoulders and tapered waist. "You look pretty good yourself."

"Hmmm. Dinner isn't for another half hour. I need to steal you away for a few minutes. Official business."

Although I could barely see his face behind the simple black mask, there was mischief in his chocolate-brown eyes. "What if I'm needed?"

"You're definitely needed." We snuck away to the elevator and up to his office.

"This is dangerous, Trent. We should be downstairs," I said as he pulled me to his desk.

"Everyone is fully engaged in the party, and I can't wait another minute to live out the biggest fantasy I've had since you walked into this room." He sat me on the edge of his desk and kissed me while his fingers danced along the front of my dress. "You're too damn tempting. I told myself I'd wait until later tonight, but I need to have you now."

It was wrong to be locked away in his office during the party, but I couldn't resist the way he made me feel. I couldn't tell him no. I should have... I really should have, but I couldn't. Instead, I let him pull my dress down and suck on my breasts. The sensation went right to my core. My body tingled and clenched, more than aware of what was to come. "Don't mess up my hair," I muttered. I should have been more concerned about getting caught but couldn't bring myself to care.

"Wouldn't dream of it," he mumbled around my breast. Trent pulled the top of my dress back in place and flipped me around. With a hand on my back, he pressed my chest to the desk. "This is going to be fast and furious. I'll make it up to you later." He tugged my dress up around my hips as my fingers splayed against the hard surface. Within seconds, he kicked my legs apart and pushed inside me.

"Oh, shit, Trent!" One hand snaked around the front of me and played with my clit as he pounded into me from behind. It wasn't sensual or sweet. It was down and dirty fucking and I loved it!

"Come for me, Gia. I'm not going to last long." He pinched my clit, and it was game over. I went soaring into the abyss of ecstasy. Sparks erupted and flowed to every part of my body, making my fingers and toes tingle while my pussy clasped tight around his cock. With a few more thrusts, he fell over the edge with me, letting out a growl as he collapsed over my back. "Fuck, that was amazing," he gasped in my ear. "Are you okay?"

Besides being squished between him and the desk, I was perfect. "I'm good." Trent pushed himself to standing, slipped my panties back in place, and pulled my dress down over my hips, letting it fall to the floor. I grabbed my purse from where I'd dropped it and headed to the connected bathroom for a quick touch-up. Lifting my mask, I inspected myself in the mirror. Besides my cheeks being flushed, no one would be the wiser that I'd just had sex on my boss's desk. I tucked a stray curl back into place, lowered my mask, and reapplied my lipstick. *Good as new.*

Trent stepped behind me. "What's the damage?"

I smiled at him. "A bruised hip bone, but I think I'll survive." I straightened his bow tie. "Why don't you head down first. I'll be right behind you."

He gave me a kiss on the cheek, sparing my freshly applied lipstick. "Don't be long."

"I won't. I promise." After Trent left, I used the restroom and double-checked myself in the mirror. This night was going better than I could have ever expected. I just needed to get through dinner and the speech, and then I was home free. Quickly checking the online app for the silent auction, I gasped. We'd made more money than I would make in a lifetime and the night wasn't over yet.

I hightailed it back to the party, anxious to tell Trent about our success.

"There she is. The lady of the hour," Trent's dad said.

Sitting at our table were Trent's mom and dad, Brett and Penny, Hunter and a busty blond, Trent, and myself. Scooting into the empty seat next to Trent, I said, "I was checking the silent auction. It's a huge success."

Rose piped up, "Of course it is, dear. Everything is simply perfect. I dare to say you and Trent make a great duo. I'm anxious to see what else you two pull out of your hats."

"It was mostly Gia," Trent said.

"That's not true. Penny is my right-hand gal and Brett helped too. It was truly a team effort."

Rose glanced at Trent's brother. "Did you help also?"

Hunter cleared his throat. "Maybe you forgot, but I was in Albuquerque for almost a month. It's hard to help when you're in a different state." He glared at Trent. "Seems all the magic happened when I was away."

I squirmed in my chair. The only good thing about Hunter being at our table was the blond attached to his arm. She giggled a lot and practically sat in Hunter's lap, but at least his focus was off me. Perhaps he was true to his word and moved on.

Chapter 30
Trent

Dinner was uneventful, as my parents entertained us with highlights of their trip. When the dishes were cleared away, it was time for Gia to make her speech. I squeezed her knee under the table and whispered, "You'll be great."

She strode to the podium in her three-inch heels and took a deep breath. "Good evening, ladies and gentlemen. My name is Gia Romano and I'm the director of entertainment and events here at Mystique. I want to thank you all for spending your evening with us. Each year we choose a worthy cause to support, and this year is no exception. There's a secret hiding in our community that no one wants to talk about. One out of every three women has been a victim of domestic abuse. These women are not strangers... they're sisters, mothers, aunts, cousins, friends, and neighbors."

She went on to tell the stories of brave women who shared their experiences with her. As I watched Gia, I was in awe. You'd never know she was as nervous as a mouse in a cage full of lions. Her confidence shined through with every word she spoke. I felt the sincerity in her voice as she advocated for the women of Las Vegas.

"So, join me in unmasking domestic abuse. We can no longer let the victims hide in the shadows under a coat of shame. It's time to bring light to the issue." Gia reached behind her head and untied the satin laces, removing her mask and pausing while the guests did the same. "These women aren't looking for a handout, they're looking for a way out. So, open your hearts… and your wallets… and let's make a difference."

The room erupted in a standing ovation of thunderous applause. Gia waited for it to die down, then held up her hand. "There's one more thing… this is a party, so I want to see everyone on the dance floor. Drink, be merry, and don't forget to check out the silent auction if you haven't done so. Enjoy your evening."

I placed my mask on the table and watched her walk off the stage. She looked phenomenal in the emerald-green sequined dress that accentuated all my favorite parts. One long leg peeked out of the slit, enough skin showing to drive me crazy. She was damn lucky I didn't rip the thing completely off her in my office. My self-control was good, but it was being tested by the minute.

My mother intercepted Gia and enveloped her. I couldn't hear what was being said, but the smile on Gia's face said enough. Seeing the two of them together, chatting and laughing, pulled at my heartstrings. It'd been a long time since I introduced my mother to someone I dated. The glory of this was she already liked Gia and had no idea we were together.

"She's a keeper," my dad said as he nudged me with his shoulder.

"That she is," I answered. "Did I tell you she closed the Ariel Fox deal? It's a trial residency, but if everything goes well, it could mean big revenue for Mystique."

"Damn. Your mother is rarely wrong, but she was spot on with hiring Gia. She's a shark."

"Which one? Mom or Gia?"

"I'd venture to say both." My dad chuckled. "Now, if you'll excuse me, I'm going to spin my wife around the dance floor." I hadn't seen my mom and dad dance together in years. Apparently, their little trip brought back that lovin' feeling.

Gia strode over with a hand on her chest. "I'm so glad that's over. I was nervous as hell up there."

"No one would ever know. You looked cool as a cucumber." I held out my arm. "Would you do me the honor of dancing with me, Miss Romano?"

Gia hooked her arm with mine. "Mr. Dorsey, I'd love to dance with you."

The music slowed to a sultry rhythm as I led her into the mass of people. With one hand twined with hers and the other around her waist, I held Gia far enough away to be respectable. "The next time I dance with you, everyone will know you're mine. I'm telling my father on Monday we're together. No more hiding in the shadows. It's time to unmask our relationship."

She gulped. "So, we're a couple? You and me? What if he doesn't approve? What if we both lose our jobs?" Every worry she had came out in a steady stream.

"My father has all but already said he approves. He's very impressed with everything you've done in the past couple months. No one will question your ability."

"Promise?" The vulnerability in her voice nearly killed me.

"You have nothing to worry about."

I woke the next morning with my body wrapped around Gia. We'd stayed until the end of the fundraiser, making sure to thank our guests for their generous donations that far exceeded our goal. Then, I brought her back to my apartment, where I more than made up for the hasty fuck in my office.

Gia stretched, rubbing her ass against my cock. "Good morning," she mumbled.

"Good morning, sunshine." I pressed my body against her soft curves. "How do you feel?"

She rolled so we were face to face. "Tired. Sore. Happy."

I brushed a strand of red hair behind her ear. "How happy?"

"Very"

Every fear I had before floated away when I was with her. "I forgot to tell you something last night."

"Yeah? What's that?" She rubbed her fingers along my beard.

"I like you being here."

She giggled. "Well, I like being here."

"That's good because I'd like to make it permanent. I'm in love with you, Gia. Move in with me."

Her eyes went wide then softened. "Say it again."

"Move in with me."

She slapped me on the arm. "Not that part."

I held her face in the palm of my hand. "I love you, Gia. I want to spend all my days and nights with you."

"I love you too, Trent. I have for a while, but I was too afraid to tell you. I wasn't sure it was real."

I rolled her over and pinned her wrists to the mattress, looking right into her gorgeous blue eyes. "I'm totally in love with you. It's real. You're the most real thing that's ever come into my life. I've never felt this way about anyone before. This going back and forth between our places is killing me. No more sneaking around. Be with me."

"I love you too, but you're going to get sick of me if we're working and living together."

"Not a chance. There's plenty of space and you can keep the hotel room if you need to get away from me. I don't want to go another day waking up without you by my side."

"I'm not a good cook."

"I don't give a fuck about that.

"I snore."

I laughed. "I'm aware."

"I have a lot of clothes."

"I have big closets.

"This isn't my real hair color," she blurted.

I nuzzled my nose into her neck. "I figured, but it's not your hair I'm in love with. I don't care if it's red, brown, blond, or black. Quit making excuses and say yes."

She bit her lip and nodded. "Yes."

"Finally." I pressed my lips to hers and tangled our tongues together. She made me the happiest man in the world with one simple word. There was nothing that was going to keep me away from this woman.

Chapter 31
Gia

My phone pinged from where it sat on the nightstand. It was the third time in the last few minutes. I looked over at Trent, who was still sound asleep. Dawn was barely breaking, the sky a bluish gray, which meant we had at least another hour before getting me back to Mystique to shower and change for work. After today, there'd be no more back and forth. I'd be able to relax and drink my coffee on the balcony.

I settled into the silk sheets. Whoever was trying to reach me could wait. *Ping!*

"For Christ's sake," I mumbled. There was no sense in trying to go back to sleep. I grabbed my phone and went out to the front room so it didn't wake Trent. It rang and Penny's name popped up on the screen. "It's too early," I answered with a yawn.

"Sorry. Did you see my messages?"

"Not yet. What is it?"

"You need to look right now. I'll wait."

I clicked into my text messages.

Penny: Are you awake?

Penny: Wake up!
Penny: We've got a problem!!!!

The last message had a link attached. I clicked on it and watched in horror. "Oh, my god!"

"Gia? Gia? Talk to me!"

I lifted the phone to my ear. "How?"

"It came through my email a few minutes ago. It was sent to everyone in our office."

Shock. I was definitely in shock. "Who? How?"

"It came from Trent."

I looked back to the bedroom. "But I've been with him all night."

"I don't know, girl."

My head spun. There was no way. I'd been played. "How quick can you pick me up from Trent's?"

"I can be there in ten minutes."

"I'll meet you out front."

I gambled my reputation, my job, and my heart… and I lost everything.

Chapter 32
Trent

I rolled over and reached for Gia only to find the sheets cold and empty. *Somebody was an early bird.* Stretching out on the king-size mattress, I called for her, "Hey, why didn't you wake me?"

Not getting a response, I rolled out of bed. "Gia?"

She was probably on the balcony. It seemed to be her favorite place in the apartment. I went in search of her and came up empty. She wasn't in the bathroom, the kitchen, the spare bedroom, or my office. Her purse and overnight bag were gone, as well as her toothbrush and makeup. It was as if she'd never been here at all. The only thing left was her sequined dress that hung on the back of the closet door.

Searching for my phone, I found it in the pocket of my jeans that were tossed on the floor. It was dead as a doornail. *Ugh!* I plugged it in and tried to call her, but it went immediately to voice mail.

She must have headed out early and caught a cab. It wasn't the first time, but it was going to be the last. There'd be no more of that after I talked with my father today. I hopped in the shower, got dressed, and went to work. She and I were going to have a talk about her getting in a car with strangers. It wasn't safe.

I stepped out of the elevator and was greeted by Tom. He sheepishly handed me a cup of coffee. "Your father wants to see you in his office immediately."

My father could have waited to discuss the fundraiser until after I got settled. Regardless, I needed to speak to him about Gia. There was no sense in putting it off. The sooner I told him about our relationship, the sooner I could put her mind at ease.

"Okaaay." I waved my fingers at our receptionist, Teresa, and she gave me a tight-lipped smile. It was weird.

As I walked down the hall, people scurried out of my way, barely making eye contact. I had a gruff reputation, but this was ridiculous. Not one person said hello or even looked at me.

I entered my father's office to find my mother and Hunter already there. "What the hell is going on?"

"Shut the door," my father said.

Clearly, there was an issue. "Family meeting? It's been a long time since we've had one of those." I sipped my coffee and sat next to my mother. She reached over and squeezed my hand. Again, it was odd.

My father leaned on his desk and folded his hands. "We got your email." *What?*

Reading my confusion, he continued, "As a matter of fact, everyone on this floor got it."

"I didn't send an email. To anyone." I looked between the three of them. "What's going on?"

"You really should be more careful," Hunter piped in.

My father turned his laptop toward me and pressed play on the attached video. I watched as Gia and I entered my office the night of the fundraiser. The footage was grainy, and we were wearing masks, but there was no mistaking it was us, especially with Gia's red hair. She sat on the edge of my desk. All you could see was her back, but when my head disappeared, it was obvious what was going on. I watched myself flip her over and push her chest to the desk.

Fuck! I didn't need to see any more.

My hand reached out and smacked the laptop closed. "Who's seen this?"

Hunter chuckled from his perch by the door. "Everyone."

Everyone? "I didn't send that. I didn't even make the tape! My office is supposed to be private!"

"It came from *your* email," Hunter said.

I looked between my parents. *My God! My mother watched a video of me having sex! Everyone did!* "I swear to God, I did not make that video and I certainly wouldn't share it if I had."

My mom squeezed my hand again. "We suspected you didn't."

"Then who did?" Who would do something like this, not just to me, but to Gia?

"I'm guessing the culprit is in this room." My father's gaze landed on Hunter.

Hunter? I knew he wanted my job, but he'd gone too far. I jumped out of my chair and charged, taking him to the ground. "You fucking piece of shit!" I only got one good punch in, cracking his nose again, before my father pulled me off. "Let me go!" I shook with rage.

"Sit down, Son!" my father ordered. "We're going to get to the bottom of this." He pushed me into a chair against my will and turned to Hunter. "Why?"

Hunter straightened his lapels and wiped the blood from under his nose. "I knew there was something going on between you two, but I had to prove it. Say goodbye to your job."

"What about Gia? She's going to be humiliated." I told her to trust me and I fucking failed.

"She put in her resignation this morning," my mom whispered.

She'd seen the video. That's why she ghosted me this morning. I dropped my head into my hands. This was the worst possible thing that could have happened.

"You're fired," my dad said calmly. My head snapped up, but his focus wasn't on me. It was on Hunter.

He pointed to himself. "You're firing me? He's the one who broke company policy."

My father shook his head. "What you did goes so far beyond that, not to mention illegal. You've damaged the reputation of this hotel, violated the privacy of my employees, humiliated Gia, and cost me an event coordinator."

"Gia? That's what you're worried about?" He huffed. "Pretty pieces of ass are a dime a dozen. She's totally disposable."

"She's not disposable, you stupid fuck! I'm in love with her!" It wasn't the way I imagined this conversation going, but it didn't matter.

"I knew it!" my mom exclaimed as she clapped her hands together. "I knew when I saw her at Martha's baby shower at the Onyx that she'd be perfect for you."

"Rose?" my father questioned.

My jaw dropped. "You set me up?"

She waved away my shock. "You were taking forever to settle down. A mother does what a mother has to do."

"You're in love with her?" my father asked.

"Completely. I was planning to tell you about our relationship today, but then this happened."

He gave me a soft smile. "Then you better go get her and bring her back."

"You're not firing him?" Hunter asked incredulously. "That job is supposed to be mine!"

"You have thirty minutes to clean out your office before I call security to escort you out. You've burned your last bridge with this family."

Although I would have liked to bask in Hunter's demise, I had more important things to do. "I gotta go!" I flew down the hall to Gia's office and poked my head in. Penny was taking her portraits off the wall. "Where is she?"

Penny shook her head at me in disgust. "She went home. I'm supposed to pack up her things and send them."

I pointed at her. "Don't touch another thing. I didn't do this to her, Hunter did. I'm going to bring her back. Have Tom text me every contact he has for her. I want phone numbers and addresses."

I ran to the elevators.

"Where are you going?" Penny yelled.

"To the airport!"

I was going to get her back no matter what it took.

Chapter 33
Gia

"I'll have another," I told Steve, the bartender. He was a pothead when we went to high school together. Steve bought this bar after we graduated and turned it into a thriving business.

Pothead: 1

College Graduate: 0

He placed the glass of whiskey in front of me. I choked down another sip. It was awful but effective. I wanted nothing short of drowning myself at the bottom of a bottle. Explaining my sudden reappearance in Waukegan to my family sucked. I left out all the gory details, but they knew something had gone wrong.

Gone wrong?

Well, that was the euphemism of the century. It was better than saying I got caught having sex with my boss in his office AND everyone I worked with saw the video evidence. *Fuck my life!* I took another sip of the whiskey. I was halfway to drunk and working toward completely blitzed.

"You got anything to snack on back there?" I asked Steve.

He poured peanuts into a bowl and set it on the bar. "You want me to call John?"

"Nope," I said, popping the *P*. The last person I wanted to see was my ex-husband. He'd wrap his arm around my shoulders and try to convince me to give it another go. The man put up with more shit from me than he deserved.

The door opened and a cold breeze drifted into the half-empty bar. I pulled my flannel jacket tighter around my body to ward off the chill. Spring was here, but you'd never know it. Snow covered every road in a fifty-mile radius. It was normal for the Chicago area, but a rude awakening after living in Las Vegas for the past two months.

A man sat next to me. "I'll have what she's having."

I froze and stared straight ahead, not acknowledging his presence. *What. The. Fuck?*

When Steve placed the glass on the bar, Trent picked it up and took a sip. "Your roads here are shit."

I shook the ice in my glass. "That, they are."

"And the whiskey tastes like piss."

"Sure does."

"So, what's a woman like you doing here all alone?"

Oh, this was rich! My lip quirked up. "Does that line usually work? Kind of cliché, don't you think?"

Trent quirked his head to the side. "Fair enough, but still a valid question."

"Escaping... from Vegas."

He leaned on the bar, putting us face to face. "Now, why would you want to do something like that?"

I threw my hands in the air. "Oh, I don't know! Maybe because I was involved in a sex scandal that all my coworkers now know about!" I pointed at Steve, who'd stopped midpour and stared. "Don't you fucking judge me!"

Trent grabbed my flailing arms and pinned them to my sides. "I didn't do it. It was Hunter, and he's been fired."

I struggled to get my arms free. "Well, that's just great. Everyone still saw you banging me from behind."

Steve hid his laugh behind his fist.

"I swear to God, if you tell anyone about this, I'll torch this fucking bar and watch it burn to the ground!"

Steve held his hands up and backed away. "No need to get crazy."

Trent grabbed my chin and turned my head to face him. "Do you love me, Gia?"

"Does it matter?"

"It matters. Nothing has changed. Not for me. I love you, Miss Gianna Romano. Come back to Vegas and move in with me. The job is yours if you want it."

"What about your dad?"

"He knows I have sex." Trent laughed.

I dropped my head to the bar and groaned. "I'm serious."

"So am I. It's not as bad as you think. At least none of your lady parts were showing."

"Everyone saw me orgasm," I whispered.

He pushed my hair behind my ear. "And it was beautiful. At least your parents didn't have front row-seats to the show."

"Both of them?"

"Yep." He sighed. "If we act like it's not a big deal, no one else will either. My mom loves you and my dad is pissed he's losing you. We have their support."

I shook my head. "I don't know if I can do it."

"Fine." Trent slapped the bar. "Then I'll quit and move here. Hey, bartender!" he yelled. "Are you hiring?"

Steve wiped a glass while looking Trent up and down in his three-thousand-dollar suit. "No offense, man, but we don't get many of your kind in here."

Trent shrugged. "I already met your dad. I can work with him. There's got to be something I can do."

"You met my dad?" *Fuck!* I didn't even want to know what that shit show looked like.

He nodded. "Sure did. Your mom too. How do you think I found you here?"

201

I couldn't imagine their faces when Trent showed up on their doorstep. "What did you tell them?"

"That I was in love with their daughter and needed to find her ASAP."

It was sweet. More than sweet actually, but it still didn't take away the embarrassment or humiliation.

Steve leaned on the bar between us. "Listen, Gia, this guy's obviously batshit crazy about you. Honestly, I don't see the attraction, but that's beside the point. You've been through some fucked-up stuff. So what? He's offering you a way out of this shithole. You should jump on that."

I blinked, looking between the two of them.

"What he said." Trent hiked a thumb in Steve's direction.

"I can't believe, after everything that happened, you still want me."

"Sweetheart, I flew halfway across the country, drove through a snowstorm, and drank cheap whiskey for you. If that doesn't say love, I don't know what does."

"People are going to gossip about us." I hiccuped from the booze.

He took the glass from my fingers and set it on the bar. "Fuck 'em. I'll fire them all. You're the only one who's impossible to replace. Come home with me, Gia."

Home. I always thought Waukegan was home, but my heart wasn't in Waukegan anymore. It was with Trent. Where he was, was the only place I wanted to be. A tear ran down my cheek and he swiped it away with his thumb. All my inhibitions drained away as my chest swelled for the man begging me to be by his side. "I love you too, Trent. Yes. I'll come home with you."

He pulled me from the barstool and swung me around.

Steve slow clapped. "You know what they say... What happens in Vegas stays in Vegas."

Trent dropped my feet to the floor and pressed his forehead against mine. "We happened in Vegas."

"And we're staying in Vegas." I stood on my toes and kissed him. We made out in the middle of the bar like no one was watching. I didn't care if the whole world saw us. And that kiss... it tasted like forever.

"What do you think of Elvis?" He teased.

I set my finger against his lips. "Don't press your luck."

Epilogue
2 Years Later

Everyone filed into the conference room and took their seats. My father stood at the head of the table, with my mother at his side. "The time has come to pass the torch. Rose and I have decided to leave Mystique to travel."

Grumbles echoed around the room. I couldn't blame them. My parents were great to work for and change was disconcerting, especially after decades of predictability.

My father held up his hands. "I know this is unexpected, but we're not completely disconnecting. While we travel, we'll be checking on our other properties, bringing back ideas, and keeping us competitive. Vegas is our home and Mystique is our flagship, so were not abandoning it, however we won't be as present or involved in day-to-day operations."

My mother bumped him with her hip and took over. "But fear not, we're leaving you in very capable hands. Trent and his beautiful wife, Gia, will be taking over for us."

That's right...wife. It didn't take me long to realize I needed to put a ring on it. Things were a little tense when she returned to Vegas. Our tech guy was able to get the video taken down, although it was a little late since everyone had already seen it. I walked around for weeks glaring at everyone, daring them to say two words to Gia. No one was bold or rude enough to go there. They all loved her, and I couldn't blame them. She was completely lovable. If anything, the staff was appalled the video was sent to them. They secretly applauded Hunter's removal from Mystique. Gia wasn't the first person he'd offended with his arrogance and brash behavior. No one said anything to me personally, but I heard the whispers.

I'd mellowed since Gia entered my life. My permanent scowl was replaced with what my mom called my dopey, love-struck face. I wasn't super fond of the name, but I couldn't deny I was in love with the redheaded temptress that swept me off my feet the moment I met her.

When we got married, it was in front of the fountains at the Bellagio, which my father initially objected to, but even he couldn't say no to Gia. All our friends and family joined us and not a single Elvis was present. Gia planned a spectacular reception at Mystique, pulling out all the bells and whistles.

I'll never forget what she looked like in her strapless wedding gown. It hugged her in all the right places and showed off her phenomenal figure. It took everything I had not to whisk her away to my office for a quick romp, but we learned our lesson the hard way. Turned out Hunter had put a hidden camera by the pictures on the shelf in my office. The weasel had been watching us the entire time. Gia and I agreed to no more sex in public places, no matter how private they appeared. The video of us could have been so much worse and neither of us was willing to risk the consequences.

My father cleared his throat, bringing me back to the here and now. I stepped to the head of the table and held my hand out for Gia to join me. I wrapped my arm around her waist as a show of affection and solidarity. "Taking over Mystique is both an honor and a privilege. I assure you we have no intentions of changing what works but only want to make things better."

"I do have one pet project I've been working on," Gia said. "Starting next month, we'll be offering free in-house childcare for all employees." A round of whoops came from the women and a few of the men too.

205

"I'm gonna be a grandma!" my mom blurted, then quickly covered her mouth. "Sorry."

Gia laughed. "It's fine, Rose. I couldn't hide it much longer anyway." She rubbed her barely-there bump. "We're having a baby."

"Boy or girl?" Genevieve asked.

"We don't know yet," I answered. My hope was for a boy, because the thought of having a mini Gia running around as a teenager gave me heart palpitations.

"Could be one of each," Gia said. "Twins run on my mom's side of the family."

I'm pretty sure my heart stopped completely. "What? How come I'm just learning this now?"

She shrugged. "Guess it never really came up."

Everyone laughed at my expense. I was barely ready for one, let alone two. "But we'd know by now, right?" Seemed like a conversation that should have been had alone instead of in front of the staff.

My mom hugged Gia. "Doesn't matter. As long as the baby or babies are healthy. I'm so excited!"

I pulled my shit together and addressed the room again. "Because I'll be taking the position as CEO, Gia will become COO and head of public relations and marketing." I motioned for Penny to stand up. "Our new director of entertainment and events has more than earned the position."

Penny gave everyone a little wave with one hand and placed the other on her very obvious protruding belly. She and Brett snuck off and eloped to Hawaii two months before our wedding without a word to anyone.

But we could hardly be mad. Everyone was entitled to their secrets. That's part of what made Sin City so alluring.

And ours was the biggest secret of all. Two devilishly handsome guys, one beautiful redheaded temptress, and a crazy twist of fate.

Who would have thought one night could change everything?

Don't miss Brett & Penny's steamy story in
Billionaire Bachelor in Vegas.

Want to know everything that happened between Gia, Trent, and Brett during their sexy ménage à trois? Get the ***exclusive extended prologue*** for free by signing up for my newsletter. This is the only place it's available!

www.subscribepage.com/whathappensinvegasextendedprologue

Thank you so much for choosing to read ***What Happens in Vegas.*** If you enjoyed the story, please leave a review on Amazon, Goodreads, or BookBub. They help so much!

Don't Want to Say Goodbye?

Check Out My Other Books:

Hearts Trilogy
Hearts on Fire
Shattered Hearts
Reviving my Heart

Wild Hearts Trilogy
Wild Hearts
Secrets of the Heart
Eternal Hearts

Forever Inked Novels
Tattooed Hearts: Tattooed Duet #1
Tattooed Souls: Tattooed Duet #2
Smoke and Mirrors
Regret and Redemption
Sin and Salvation

Vegas Love Series
What Happens in Vegas
Billionaire Bachelor in Vegas

Acknowledgments

Thank you for choosing to read **What Happens in Vegas**. I loved telling the story of Gia and Trent. This book was originally part of the Hot Vegas Nights series. It was out of my normal realm, as it was my first time doing a multi-author collaboration. I enjoyed working with these talented ladies to bring you Hot Vegas Nights. They are true professionals, wonderful cheerleaders, and a superior support team. A special thank you to S.L. Sterling for organizing the project and bringing us all together.

To the Hot Vegas Nights ladies~ Thank you for including me on this project. I've enjoyed your friendship and getting to know you gals. It was fun sharing ideas and interconnecting our books. Best of luck to whatever your futures hold.

To my husband~ I could have never done this without your love and support. Thank you for affording me the opportunity to do what I really love. Not many people get the chance to retire from their job to pursue their passion. For that I will be forever grateful. Also, technology scares the crap out of me, and you've been a patient saint walking me through all my mishaps and frustrations. Thank you for believing in me!

To Linda, Ari, Missie, Heather, and Kat~ You ladies are the best beta readers anyone could ask for! You've supported my journey and given me pep when mine was all gone. Your suggestions, critiques, and encouragement helped me in ways you'll never understand. Your constructive criticism improved this book so much and helped make it into something I'm proud of. I could never thank you all enough for your help!

To my readers~ Thank you for supporting me in this journey. There are thousands of books that you could have chosen to read, and I am honored you chose mine. Please spread the word and leave a quick review on Amazon, Goodreads, or BookBub if you have enjoyed this book. Without you, writing would still be a dream.

About the Author

Sabrina Wagner writes sweet, sassy, sexy romance novels featuring tattooed men and the strong women who challenge them. She's been obsessed with reading romance since middle school and began writing in 2016. After twenty-six years of being an elementary school teacher, she left the classroom and began writing fulltime. Now she spends her time crafting steamy stories about stubborn, alpha men and the sassy women who bring them to their knees.

Sabrina lives in Michigan with her true-life, alpha-hero husband. She has two twenty-something children and two adorable cats, Olive and Moo. Sabrina thrives off caffeine, enjoys spending time with her family, and loves basking in the sun. It's rare to find her without a book in her hand or a story spinning through her head.

Sabrina believes true friends should be treasured, a woman's strength is forged by the fire of affliction, and everyone deserves a happy ending. She enjoys spending time with her family, cuddling her kittens, walking on the beach, and of course, reading. Sabrina is a hopeless romantic and knows all too well that life is full of twists and turns, but the bumpy road is what leads to our true destination.

Want to be the first to learn book news, updates and more?
Sign up for her Newsletter.
https://www.subscribepage.com/sabrinawagnernewsletter

Printed in Great Britain
by Amazon

41812606R00126